WHITEOUT

A CHRISTIAN CRIME THRILLER

Winter keeps secrets.
Some, deadly.

BOOK 1
Carter Jons

Whiteout - A Christian Crime Thriller

Copyright © 2023 Wayne C. Stewart

waynecstewart.com
Email: wayne.stewart@waynecstewart.com

Author Wayne C Stewart facebook page:
facebook.com/authorwaynecstewart/

I waited patiently for the LORD;
he turned to me and heard my cry.
He lifted me out of the slimy pit,
out of the mud and mire;
he set my feet on a rock
and gave me a firm place to stand.
He put a new song in my mouth,
a hymn of praise to our God.
Many will see and fear the LORD
and put their trust in him.

Psalms 40:1-3

ONE

Rookie Iowa State Trooper Carter Jons drew the short straw.

The winter storm warning wasn't enough to convince midwesterners to stay home, even if Interstate 80 nearing Omaha had been nearly impassable much of the last three hours. The Pottawattamie County Sheriff's department was short-staffed, so veteran cohorts from both agencies policed the highway and side roads as even hearty drivers were slowed to a crawl. Jons had the harder, even slower assignment, ambling solo through McClelland, a stoic town of 151 souls on the two-lane G61, another 40 minutes southwest. Heavy flakes condensed into solid mass. Each wiper cycle—a good shoveling.

White out.

Trooper Jons slowed to ten, floodlights on full, doing his best just to stay on the pavement. Were someone in trouble on this forlorn road he may be able to assist, that is if he saw them in time. Currently, visibility beyond the roadside ditch was dependent solely on the vagaries of wind and white.

Two faded headlights appeared out of nowhere, just off his left front bumper. A sudden spray of snow and ice rose up and over the hood and windshield and Carter pulled hard right. Reaching for the horn, his left hand missed, sliding by and grabbing the wheel on its rebound. Mashing brakes, the cruiser did as ordered, skidding to a stop just shy of a five-foot embankment.

That was way too close.

A breath. A beat. Jons grabbed his radio handset.

"District 3 dispatch, this is Jons, G61 rural check. Some idiot just ran me near into the culvert. Car is running and," he paused, "... all sounds ok. Need a visual check before proceeding."

"District 3 Dispatch, 10-4. Carter, you having trouble with the locals again?"

"Yeah, check. You know me. All about the drama."

"Alright, just keep everything in front of you and let us know when you're on the way."

Carter swore he heard background snickering.

"Will do. Jons out."

Carter stepped outside, wincing and pulling his fur-lined long coat up to cover the back of his neck. These first few feet were the worst conditions imaginable. A thousand tiny prickles of ice struck his face, the only still-exposed part of his flesh. Every step shortened. Each movement condensed. The last thing he needed was a fall and then endless ribbing back at District.

A first-year patrolman, Carter was trying his best to establish good momentum in a new vocation. He'd taken all the extra shifts. No sick days, even when he was legit ill. Sure, he was a newb. But he was going to be the very best newb possible. Just like this assignment; no arguments. Every time he got in the car he got better. That's what mattered.

Jons walked around the front of the cruiser.

Lights. Grill. Hood. Alignment.

A cracking sound in the distance.

His head snapped around.

What was that?

Carter turned, the sound quickly overcome by both wind and engine. He pulled back his massive coat hood, cupping his ears. Still no understanding. It was far too cold to keep his head out in the open. Five steps back to the car, Carter reached in and turned the key. Engine off, lights on, flooding the empty field. A small, odd forest stood out among endless acreage. Windbreaks and ecosystem buffers. Farmers a hundred years ago had figured that one out.

He edged along the car body, then down and through the ditch. Ascending the other side, the sound returned as a massive evergreen snapped in the distance, four or five of its largest branches crashing down to meet the whitened surface with a hush.

Too much weight.

Frost had charmed the trees these last few weeks. The accumulation couldn't remain forever. It was only a matter of time.

Alright then.

A few snapped branches. Case closed.

Carter made his way back to the safety of the front seat, kicked snow off his boots, and closed the door. Flashers on, he headed back with a report of nothing to report.

TWO

Twenty-two-year-old Justyn Banks lay trapped, upside-down, in his vehicle's now-compromised interior.

T he near miss on the two-lane had sent him careening down the snowy road and mistaking a farm service track for the main pavement. He'd seen the small bridge and the drop, coming at him with no way to stop. A massive overcorrection slid him ever closer to the edge of an unusually deep creekbed. The van's weight teetered. But then physics took over and the young man felt as if the world were turning upside down. It was, at least for him.

The first drop was sickening. The resulting damage, shocking. Pressing in, torn and sharpened edges of metal and glass threatened from every angle. Retreating from the spider-webbed windshield, eyes tight, arms across chest with hands covering his face, he rotated as hard left as possible, only to realize the side windows would do just as much damage. Pick your poison. Upturned and constrained, panic gripped the young man like the belts at his shoulder and waist. Gravity commanded, unrelenting. The buckle and clasp were bent and cemented in place.

So he stopped. Listened.

Weather pummeled the van's exterior, ice and snow attempting to breach its already weakened body. Beyond the call of howling winds, the engine spat. Then, the choking and awkward rhythm of damaged pistons, belts, and hoses settled to a single, most ominous sound: the steady release of fuel from reservoir to engine block.

Drip.

Drip.

Drip.

So rhythmic.

A timer, counting down.

Justyn anticipated an explosion and then a million tiny projectiles, followed by one final instant of pain. Uneven breaths racked his torso. Spasms and then heaving. Seconds bled and Justyn's pulse overwhelmed, threatening exit via his temples.

More drips. More time.

But, nothing.

Still, nothing. Except…

Drip.

Drip.

Drip.

Fear crested, an unstoppable wave. Justyn released an empty scream: hollow, wordless.

He dizzied.

And then, black.

Sometime later the van dropped another few feet. The sensation shook Justyn awake. He listened again. No more dripping. No winter's fury. No sounds at all, just radio static announcing his good fortune.

Clarity washed over the young man. He dared open his eyes.

I'm not ready.

Not yet.

THREE

District 3 coffee was horrendous. But at least it was warm.

From his state-issued green metal desk, Carter wondered whether the next sip was worth it.

"Make sure you spell *evergreen* correct, Jons. I mean, after it scared you like that, you might still be a little shaky."

"Nice. Thanks. Thanks very much."

District 3 wonderkid Amy Bradford smirked. She'd catapulted straight out of undergrad and through the academy with honors. Law enforcement was in her blood. Three generations. All the way back to grandad, a legend in small town Arkansas police lore, and for good reason. The first black sheriff in their very southern county, his family's ascension from plantation to badge was nothing short of remarkable. Barely 30, she reminded Carter of her five years seniority at every opportunity.

Carter, on the other hand, was 42 and looking to make up lost time but not longing for leadership. He'd had plenty of that in his previous job. Hadn't turned out very well. Long hours and burdensome toil didn't pay off the way you'd imagine. In the end, he still got fired. Plenty of folks thought it was unfair. It was. But that doesn't matter. Workplace politics trump all.

Even in a church.

"Or maybe," Bradford turned again. "Maybe you could preach at those unruly trees? Go back and let them know they're *Gawwwwwd's* handiwork and all will be well? Better yet, a couple of sentences in your report about how we're all like those branches. Overburdened. Ready to break. In need of releeeeeease!" Her southern sermon style played impeccably, right down to the elongated vowels and uplifted end tone.

Cheers and clapping rose throughout the small shift room. Some cringed at the revival play-along but still found it funny.

Carter mostly agreed.

"I must admit," he started. "My years of theological training have prepared me for this very moment. But, yet," he halted. "Instead, I will simply drink this," his hand raised the mug. "Very. Bitter. Cup."

Groans.

Feet shuffled. Chairs creaked as the troopers returned to their desk work.

Carter's self-satisfaction lasted only a moment. A small subscreen appeared on his desktop monitor, alongside his nearly complete report of what would become known as the *Tragic Tree Affair*.

Two images, side by side. Decent angle.

"You all seeing this? District 9 alert."

"Yep, something to keep an eye on," Bradford replied. "When the interstate re-opens."

The images were milemarker grabs; gray scale, grainy, poorly lit. The first, a Love's Travel Stop near Shelby, up top of the I80 run across the state and before its southern turn toward Council Bluffs and Omaha. The second was the rest stop cam at Underwood, squarely in their district's area of ops.

"Hey," a trooper across the room clarified. "Good old Ford Transit. Looks like a 2003 to me."

Everyone else waited for the explanation.

"Dad had one. Great trucks. Last forever."

"Okay," Carter chimed in. "Thanks for the ID. So," reading as best he could from the picture, "Side branding is *Buckner Feed and Seed*? Ring a bell, anyone?"

"Nope. Nice logo, though."

No's repeated. More shrugs.

Carter reviewed the first grab.

Iowa license: GBP 482.

Squinting at the second image—*Iowa License: HVH 129*—he sat back, exhaling and speaking to himself.

"Ok, Mr. Buckner. We'll need to have a little chat about why your plates changed between Shelby and Underwood."

FOUR

It was difficult to tell the time of day.

Dwindling engine heat had melted a few feet of snow pack beneath Justyn's van and it sunk into the open space carved out by the old farm's creek bed. Most of Iowa's vast fields would not have this kind of geologic form. But this part of the state had hills and valleys carved out or deposited by the last ice age. In this case, it was nearly thirty feet down from the road and bridge to the bottom of the ravine. The vehicle sat wedged midway, covered completely by another two feet of recently layered snow. Justyn, awakened by the secondary drop, had watched the slim interior light fade with every odd inch of descent. At rest for now, the cab lay in eerie entombment.

The young man instinctively reached for his phone. He caught its outline at the edges of his peripheral vision. Facedown and off. Out of reach, along with his backpack and the remains of his last fast food stop. Straining toward the ceiling, he considered the fall. From a still-upside-down position, it wouldn't be much. The roof had caved, collapsing in toward the seats and leaving only inches of headroom. The scenario was as disorienting as one might imagine. Something akin to the classic film, the *Poseidon Adventure* in which a massive ocean liner lay capsized, forcing a haggard group of survivors through battered steel and rising water levels to emerge up and out, by going ever further "down."

Justyn fingered the seatbelt clasp. Then he remembered. Bent. Jammed. He tried wiggling. The slack guide locked another half inch, as it was supposed to.

In the darkness, panic returned.

Fingertips raced over fabric, searching for weakness, something to tear. He arched and the belt lock stole another portion of mobility. More movement, evermore restriction. Energy expended. His face puffed. Blood rushed. Ears clogging.

Swirling into darkness a second time, Justyn's memories replayed a familiar scene.

———————————————

It was a small town potluck. Folding chairs. Summer heat. Everyone held a cold drink. Paper plates hosted piles of pasta. People laughed. Laughed hard.

At eleven, Justyn was a boy in-between. Too old for the kids' table. Not yet welcome with the grownups. Their mature banter always entertained. Sometimes bawdy. He snuck within earshot as the conversation turned serious.

"I don't think it's right. Not at all. What's next, we get no choice but to put up with it?"

"Well, I don't know." Justyn's father's ever-present diplomacy landed as a lighter touch among hard words. "Seems like none of our business. That's all I'm saying."

"It's *all* our business," he got in return. "Always has been. Always will be. You let them do this and we'll lose everything."

"Hey, now just wait a minute."

"No!" The temperature rose sharply. "You listen to me. This is how it always starts. Little by little. We have rights, too, you know!"

Justyn's father's face dropped. He knew better than to press, pivoting instead to a cooler topic.

The boy stepped away unseen, sipping at his pop can and meandering around the backside of the small house, the fence line, and a dog run. Fear and curiosity rose equally at the sight of the owner's dogs. Not purebreds. But good dogs. Big. Active. He kicked a few rocks and then remembered he was too old for such nonsense.

Ten minutes later the older kids gathered for football. He begged. They said no. He begged more. They relented.

Late in the game by unofficial measures, score tied, third and goal, Justyn hit his route. Bobby, sixteen, dropped back and let it go. The ball sailed over Justyn's head, through the street, and into the neighbor's yard. The youngest was always the ball boy. Even if he was in the game. He looked both ways. No cars. Two more steps.

"Do *not*," the owner's voice commanded.

Justyn froze. Obeyed. Game over.

Later in the day, embarrassment fading, Justyn approached Bobby. "Hey. What was up with that? I can cross the street, you know. Not a baby."

"What? C'mon, Justyn, you know him. He'd rather buy a new football than get it back after it's been touched by those…"

———————————————

Inside the van, the belt released, slack unfurling and heaping Justyn against the upturned metal roof.

Reality stammered. The dream lingered, heavy.

He didn't try to shake it. Didn't want to.

It was one of the most formative moments of his life. And the reason he was here, buried in a snowbank thirty minutes shy of his target.

FIVE

Cracked wallpaper was the room's best asset.

C live Richards pulled the laptop closer and checked his email. *Where are you, you little brat?* Justyn was late checking in. Again. Better not be playing those stupid games online. This is not a joke. Not a drill.

Richards got up, pacing the room. He wasn't a believer. Didn't care about the cause. Pulled in as the professional his shadowy employers didn't have, his presence was pragmatic. He had skills. Nothing more. And he was for sure not going to miss a big payday because of some ridiculous acolyte.

7pm.

Dark for a couple hours now. Always that way this time of year. Depressing. But at least it would provide cover. Checking the real world of their schedule and operational environment was necessary. Nighttime made for better rehearsal. Rehearsal was simple: meet up south of town and go over the plan. And then go over the plan some more. Justyn had better get his act together.

An hour later, Richards pushed the mostly clean plate forward, a few fries remaining. *The Dew Drop Inn* was one of those greasy spoons you needed to experience at least once. He'd spent far more time than that in clones across the country. Out of the way. Easy in and out. The meat and starches would get him through the evening.

Sitting at 10th and Pierce, the restaurant lay a mile from the underpass of Interstate 480, their operational intersect. Leaving an average tip, and in no apparent hurry, Richards pulled his nondescript rental car out, through a random series of turns, and into the backlot of *DJ's Dugout and Sportsbar*. The rest of the way would be on foot. Foul weather had its upside in this business. Most people — for good reason — stayed home, inoculated from the world in which he lived and breathed. All good, so far.

The mighty *Missouri* painted state lines between Iowa and Nebraska, nestled astride urban fringe and Richards' building of interest, *CHI Health Center Arena*, itself neatly occupying the space between waterfront and highway. Her 18,000 seats hosted major sporting and entertainment events, notably Creighton University Men's Basketball. Meca Drive, north of the stadium, would be the way in. He'd reviewed their documents earlier, waiting for Justyn to show. The IDs were good. Really good. Unbelievably good. It was better to not know, but someone important was running that end of the op. Approaching from the river, a hundred yards off, Richards mentally redrew the setup, as he had a hundred times in his head and on paper.

Bank's van carried half the package. His, the other half.

When the kid arrived they had a day to get things ready. New signs on the truck. An unremarkable facilities contractor. They'd be inside hours before start time and if all went as planned, halfway across the state when it all came crashing down.

Richards paced some more, keeping to cover as much as he could. He'd gotten good at hip shots with his phone. The angles weren't great but they provided basic intel revealed only by imagery. His memory was decent. Still, best not to trust it beyond reasonable expectations. From three-hundred feet away he captured the entire building. Entrances. Exits. There would be lots of people. Not many ways in or out.

Especially in a hurry.

Slipping the phone into his overcoat pocket, he lit a cigarette and cupped his hands for warmth.

Just another guy on a cold night in Omaha.

"Hey."

Richards turned, reaching casually into his pocket toward the long, slender, knife.

"Spare a bro some coin?"

So young. Couldn't be more than twenty. Next-generation vagrancy.

"Sure," Richards released the blade and reached for his money clip. "I got a few bucks. Take care. You cold? Need a smoke?"

"Nah. Can't do the nic, man. But thanks for the cash."

Quick. Nonchalant. He'd be far more forgettable if he just took care of it and moved on. The very last thing he needed was a youthful indigent providing clues for his capture. Poetic, yes, but not his plan. Richards lit another cigarette and started back to the hotel. With tonight's rehearsal over, his reverse route was just as unpredictable.

As he preferred.

Upon return, the forty-five dollar-a-night room had not improved.

Richards dropped the money clip, knife, and Beretta M9 onto the side table and opened a laptop. Within a minute, he'd chosen a template and the list. This one would go out as a leather goods sale. Twenty-eight-thousand recipients. Not a single one had signed up for the email blast.

Except for Justyn.

Send.

While not prone to anxiousness, he could not complete this job the way he wanted without the young man. Or at least a replacement. And the time horizon for that was dwindling fast. Maybe the universe was telling him to just walk away and retire somewhere sunny and warm? Aruba? Those TV ads were tempting. But a message from the great beyond waving him off the job? Not likely. The man had seen enough in this life to disregard any kind of destiny or even simple cohesion beyond the basics. Get yours. Take from someone else if necessary. Live another day. Justyn's silence was troubling but would neither rob him of sleep nor entice him to trust anyone besides himself.

Laying back on the stone-hard bed, he pulled up images from the earlier recon. Sure enough, those stairs and ramps would be their undoing. Not his concern. Instead, he focused elsewhere.

Entrances.

Service Roads.

Exit route.

And last, the arena marquee.

Friday, 7pm. Justice Now: A Call to Racial Reconciliation.

SIX

The case of the switched plates had only gotten murkier.

C arter leaned over the small home office desk. Hands folded, his eyes fell, unfocused, toward the bottom edge of the screen. Slowed breaths belied frustration, both at the question before him and those waiting in line.

One set of plates farther north. A new set approaching Omaha. Buckner Feed & Seed. Never heard of you. No website. No search returns at all.

Carter inhaled and then held it a beat.

"Babe... "

"*What?...* " he let it out and straightened.

"Oh, I'm sorry," Mae offered. "You were praying?"

"No. I mean, well not specifically."

The pause said everything.

Carter swiveled, resetting his attention as his wife stepped into the room. Still so beautiful. But more than that. A loveliness that ages well, portrays a life of substance, displaying dead-set conviction about their inseverable oneness.

How did I get so incredibly lucky?

"CJ," she moved closer, the abbreviation hers alone to use. "The kids are going down. Mia is reading and Theo is at the edge of his bed, waiting to catch the last train to sleepy town."

Carter smiled, half at the joy of his kids faces and the remainder self-congratulation on the creation of their family's unique nighttime ritual. At least for the younger one. Mia was far too mature at nine to abide such nonsense.

"Yeah," he replied. "Almost finished. I can wrap this up after they're down."

She tilted her head. There was something more. "Carter," this time, his full name. "They're asking again."

"Mae… "

"So, wait. Before this spins out into another argument. What *are* we doing? When is long enough? I don't know what to say anymore when it comes up."

"It's not that easy," he pulled back. "I wish I had an answer. I don't. I just don't. And the more you push me, the less I feel I can give you an answer."

"Whoa, CJ," her hands went up. "We're not talking about solving world hunger. It's just… "

"It's just *what*? You know what they did to us, to *me*. I know I should be okay with it by now, but I'm not. There. I said it. I am not okay."

"Babe," she tried softer this time. "It's just." She paused, acknowledging his pain. "It's just church."

His jaw clenched.

"And either we believe this stuff enough to re-engage… " she stepped gently.

"Or what?" he shot back.

"Or… we don't. It's kinda that simple. At least, to me. Look," she swung the chair fully in her direction. "You used to say it all the time, remember? People's profound ability to hurt each other is only bested by God's desire, and power, to heal."

Fighting his own words was a losing battle. Every single time. Thankfully, there were fewer of them now to fight. The years had helped. A new career and increased salary softened some of the bruising. Still, merely showing up at the double doors of a church building set him on fire. It was an entirely different state. Nearly five hundred miles between them. Didn't matter. *If they did it once, they could do it again.* Which made no sense at all. He was no longer a pastor. Barbs flung by a new congregation were not his to take. Or were they? And what about the bald-faced hypocrisy? Could he square what he'd always believed about God when people claiming His Name did such things? The rumors were bad enough. But outright accusations and slander?

He was stunned, shamed. Had left the only job he'd ever imagined. For no reason other than the grave sickness within every person, surfacing tragically to poison a place built on hope.

"Hey," she leaned in. "We don't need to answer this tonight. But soon, okay?"

"Yeah. Soon," he softened. "You're right. Soon."

Their lips brushed and she turned, one smooth motion toward and out the door.

Carter rotated back, his eyes sweeping across two dark bookcases before landing on the now-awakened screen. He side-glanced the cases again. The nearly-hundred volumes faded back. In lone focus lay his Bible. Second shelf, far left.

For decades the tattered blue leather held prominence on his desk, in his hands, everywhere. It wasn't for show. Carter was not a self-important man. It was a reminder. An anchor. His world had been ordered by its pages and the deep, thoughtful reflections of trusted mentors, his family, close friends. Placement on the shelf was a recent move and not as significant as it might seem. He still believed. But in the haze of pain, he was oddly putting it at arms' length. He didn't outright demote Scripture from his life. More like a little distance to salve the sting.

Love one another.

In humility value others above yourselves.

Have the same mindset as Christ Jesus.

Those words grated. Lately, it didn't take much. Pushing the "pay now" button every month on his lawyer's website did the trick. That was a huge mistake, one he'd be paying down another five years at this pace. So foolish, tens of thousands in legal fees landed as the judge found in favor of the elder board. At least the second suit seemed a possible win. He was still waiting on that.

It was insane. And then it wasn't.

His work agreement was open-ended. There was no real recourse. He worked for the board. They could dismiss him for any cause, or none at all. Lies didn't matter when it came to the law unless he waged a defamation suit, which legal advised against in no uncertain terms. The church would get a nice big check, too, covering their side of the fees. It bit hard, every budget cycle. The people he trusted had turned on him. Viciously. And he was paying for it, over and over.

"Babe?" floated in from the hallway.

"Yep," Carter replied. "Done."

He left everything where it was.

Theo's grin grew enormous the second his dad walked into the room. Almost too big for his little three-year-old face.

Carter got on hands and knees and his son jumped on his back.

"All aboard the last train to sleepy town. Making stops in Snoozeville, Snore City... "

"And Dreeeeam Junction," Theo finished.

Two more chugga-chuggas and they were at the head of the bed.

"All off at Sleepy-Town."

Theo knew the routine.

"I said, 'All *off* at Sleepy Town,'" Carter insisted, twisting and trying to dump the boy into the soft covers.

More giggles.

"I said…"

Theo slid off and into place, landing softly where the deeper cares of life would not come to call. The toddler looked so… content.

"Hey bud," Carter leaned in. "Have an awesome night. I love you. So much."

Up from his knees, a few steps down the hall, Carter took a seat on the edge of Mia's bed.

"Sweetie. Time to shut it down." A bright paperback cover caught his eye. "New book?"

"Yup."

"So, tell me the story. Good?"

"So good, Dad."

The opening question was all she needed. A verbal processor, definitely. No slowing, no breaths, until the summation was due. Once finished, she lay back, eyelids heavy.

A fatherly kiss met forehead as he brushed her hair away from her face. Sidestepping the creakiest stair boards on the way down to the kitchen, Carter approached Mae, reading at their small breakfast table.

She reached for him. "You know they were wrong, don't you? You're a good man, Carter Jons."

"Yeah, well I'm still figuring out how to be a good cop, so I need a bit more time upstairs before calling it a night."

WEDNESDAY

SEVEN

He hadn't intended to kill him.

Perry Townsend's foot lay heavy on the accelerator. He gripped the steering wheel, knuckles whitening with fear.

No, no, no, no.

He let go, palms pounding forehead, then quickly returned them to the wheel.

Honnnnnk, a semi warned as Townsend cheated Route 74's midline, just outside Idledale, Colorado. The thirty-two-year-old pulled back, eventually settling into his lane.

Stupid. So stupid.

I could have made it.

The 3am email had him up and running.

But that was two hours ago and so much had transpired.

They'd let him know he might be needed. Chances were slim. Still, be ready. Perry barely managed his anxious excitement the two previous workdays. His job was pretty good. Still, work was work. Paid the bills, few that he had. Enough for some downtime and weekend excesses. But even that he was trimming down now that he had purpose. They'd found him so much worse.

A little over three decades of life had not been kind to Townsend. His mother, try as she might, just couldn't steer clear of the things that held her, gripped her, making escape a very complicated prospect. Rehab. Jail. Rehab. More jail. Eventually, she lost hope, and with it her life. Dad was a similar story. But he just up and left. No word in some twenty-seven years. Without siblings or extended family, five-year-old Perry was suddenly and sadly orphaned.

While one would like to think the care network would do its job, kind and giving people at the helm and in every seat of influence, that was partly the story, part of the time. For some—not many— fairytale endings close the last chapter. For Townsend, it was more horror story with the one early and enduring lesson of self-reliance at all costs. But, like all such worldviews, one person, even oneself, cannot fill the void of humanity's primal internal need: identity. Belonging.

Until they came along, at just the right time.

The bender had been meant as the finale, with enough alcohol to drench each and every cell in his body, Townsend was counting on the poisoning to take its toll without him being conscious. A full eighteen hours later he woke, feeling like he had died for real. The pain was excruciating as his liver and kidneys fought back hard. He couldn't think straight, too much of the chemical depressant still flooding his gray matter. He could see, barely. He was in a hospital room. Tubes everywhere. Charts. Beeping. And at his bedside.

Them.

Three of them. Genuinely concerned and not going anywhere soon.

Perry caught the exit for 470 South.

Those few frantic moments escaping the small town west of Denver left another ten hours to target. That is, if the weather, and law enforcement, cooperated. He'd calmed enough to think now. It was a good thing his route had been predetermined: follow 470 away from Denver proper, meet up with I70 eastward and then 70, north out of Topeka. He was certain he'd make more mistakes if it wasn't as spelled out. Mistakes he did not want to make.

I will not let you down, brothers.

The thought surprised, but not in a bad way.

Three years had come and gone since the day they took him in, paying his medical bills, setting him up with work and a new place to live. The transformation happened gradually. Their ideas, not completely foreign, took a while to sink in. But there was also a certain symmetry to it all. Townsend had been hurt by people. Often, people in groups. There was a sense in which his defense mechanisms were primed for gentle redirection. The distance from "someone" hurt me to "they" hurt me is a surprisingly short venture. Perry was not innocent, especially now. But he was a victim, of that there was no doubt.

The distance gained from Idledale allowed him to recount his steps. They'd want to know for sure he wasn't compromised. That he could complete his part of the mission. So he forced himself to relive the last, early hours.

He flashed back to the van pick-up. It had been in the self-storage unit, just like they said. The overnight staff was a brother. No problem there.

The restaurant.

That shouldn't have happened. But it was the middle of the night and once en route, he wouldn't be able to stop, not even to pee. The brothers had welded a second gas tank onto the van's underside, giving him the range needed for a nonstop trip to target. He only stayed fifteen minutes. Even parked the van two blocks away.

Mistake one.

The pancakes had settled without warning. So tired. *Another fifteen minutes, that's all I need.*

Mistake two.

He'd even set his phone alarm. At least he thought he had, until the loud knocking on his driver-side window forced him awake almost two hours later, noticing the alarm time had been entered but the "on" slider had not been activated. The owner of the small machine shop had some questions as to the contents of Perry's van.

The rear door latch? Perry considered and then lamented.

Mistake three.

Townsend tried to skip through the next set of memories, cringing at who he had become in those few anxious moments. Still, he needed to be clear as to his steps. No blood on the vehicle. Body in the ravine, heavy brush. No footprints leading the way. These concerns came not from experience. Just seemed the right thing. Maybe too many crime shows. Maybe just enough. The cover of pre-dawn and the quiet of the small town told him he'd been successful. So he secured the cargo door, got back into the cab and headed out.

Four mistakes.

He was, even after they had welcomed him in, after all they done for him, still such a screw-up. But this was different. In his former life, he'd run. That was because he didn't have anything. Anyone. Now he had a family. This family had a cause. He would not make mistake five.

Just past Buckley AFB Townsend caught I70. Ten over the limit the last half hour, it was okay now to slow down a bit.

Perry counted on the next long hours to be uneventful, even while keeping his eyes on road and mirrors. Last night's snows had been plowed and he moved eastward on dry, reddish pavement. The sun crested. It had been a rocky start on the road to triumph. Now, all he could do was trust the plan. Trust his people. Trust his beliefs.

EIGHT

District 3's small briefing room overflowed with troopers.

They'd heard much of this before. Still, Homeland Security raising its National Terrorist Advisory wasn't something to easily dismiss.

"For now, we continue to assess that the primary threat of mass casualty violence in the United States stems from lone offenders and small groups motivated by a range of ideological beliefs and/or personal grievances."

Carter waited for more. Instead, he got a Homeland Security Seal fading to black.

"Perfect," one of the more senior troopers started.

Bradford couldn't let it go. "What's that supposed to mean?"

The trooper waited, not knowing if he wanted to start the day this way or not. He hadn't slept well. Why not.

"Come on, Bradford. Same old song and dance from HomeSec. Broad threat assessment that never goes away. Never anything actionable. Seems like," he pointed to the printout they'd been handed "… lots of crying wolf with this administration. What? Going on 16 months now? The same advisory. Same bullet points. Same case and no way to solve it."

"So," Bradford shot back. "Three school shootings. A mall. The cultural organization. The club. Just coincidence, right? Nothing to see here. Move on."

"Hey, cool it, junior high. No one likes the world we live in when we look at that list. But you know what's missing just as much as I do. That assessment is so lopsided, it couldn't hold another shovel full. Maybe it would help if they listed *everything*. We've all seen it. Cases, unresolved, or a motivation that doesn't fit the scenario. And the international stuff is now just a bunch of opportunists? Like they didn't have evil plans until we started our own battles. Everything starts and ends with us only? That's a stretch and you know it."

"What I know," Bradford returned, "is that you don't know what you don't know."

"I'm with Wagner on this," Carter jumped in.

Bradford's glare couldn't have bored any deeper. Still, a measure of self-control remained that comes only from repeating this line of questioning and its always disappointing outcomes.

"You see anomalies, right?" she pressed.

"Well, yeah," Carter replied. "The math is not that hard. Violent crime itself is an anomaly, statistically speaking. Ideologically-motivated violent crime doesn't even register, not to mention the challenge of making a strong enough correlation with the motivation and not just the act. Most of the planet basically gets along, doing its thing day by day and staying out of each other's way. Sometimes we actually enjoy each other."

"Sounds like you're in the wrong line of work, preacher."

"No, don't get me wrong. That's the point. I'm here because of the anomalies. But to say that every day we face existential threat as a community, a state, or even a nation is just so much overheated rhetoric—it's really out of control."

"So, we're all good, then? Kumbaya? All the bright people at HomeSec are just pawns and propagandists."

"I have no idea, Bradford. Wouldn't even try to answer that one in any way that might be helpful or accurate. What I do know is that it feels like most of what comes at us these days is a call to either fear or anger. Not just government. News. Social media. The messages we hear every day are telling us we should either build a bunker or burn it all down. Those don't seem like great choices. Certainly not sustainable."

She pointed aggressively. "You don't know what people can do."

"Now, there," Carter replied a little sharper than intended. "You're very wrong."

Three rectangular tables. The kind every church has. Heavy, pressed board with a laminate top. Chips at the edges. Ten men sat at the unevenly padded folding chairs. Nearly all of them had their arms folded as well.

"Pastor," the Elder Chair began. "We've been reviewing the books. We spent how much?…"

A bespeckled man reviewed his spreadsheet and then spoke up. "Thirty-five-hundred-twenty-three. And fifteen cents."

"Thank you, Carl."

He paused.

"And this went directly to First Methodist?"

"No," Carter spoke. "The entity was Community Reach Hope Center. First Methodist is a partner, just like us."

"That's an awful lot of money to give to another church, isn't it, pastor?"

"Uh, well, as I said, it went to the non-profit we've been a key component of for the last three years. It all went for food, clothing, housing."

"And how…" a new voice entered. "How are we making the Gospel clear to these… to the," he struggled.

"We call them clients," Carter helped.

Another elder let out a small, scoffing breath.

Carter looked his way.

"Well, clients *pay* for things," the man offered.

Don't take the bait. Don't do it.

The man only felt emboldened. "I assume we have some kind of chapel for them?"

"It's more personal than that. And there are a few ways the various churches go about it. We, I mean myself and mostly the Petersens, are at the Hope Center every other week on Monday and Thursday. People come in and we do a brief intake. Try and see what they need."

"So, that's when you share the Gospel with them?"

"Well, yeah. But it's not like we have a required talk or any kind of response for them to get help. I am a pastor, so yes, I am always looking for the opportunity to share Jesus with someone. But that's in the grocery store, at a game, wherever. And it would be super odd to make a three-point sermon a precursor to any kind of regular life interaction in those settings. How is this any different?"

Carter knew he'd said too much. Not that any of it was untrue. But his audience was clearly unimpressed.

"We pay you," the Chair started in. "… to preach. And to make hospital visits. And everything else we need done at *our* church. People's souls are at risk of eternal fire. You seem to have lost that somewhere along the way."

Yeah, but which one: the people's soul's part or the "we pay you" part.

It would feel so good to let that one out into the room.

The Chair continued. "We're very concerned here, Pastor. If you want to continue this extracurricular ministry, and use our money for it, we'll need more justification. We want to see exactly where the money is going. We want statements of faith from all the partner churches. We want a report of how many salvations each month."

Carter was astounded.

"Next item on the agenda. We have some questions about your request for a second week of paid vacation."

Bradford looked about, and read the room.

Ignorance is bliss.

"Like I said," she nodded toward the older trooper "… he doesn't know what he doesn't know. You," she turned to Carter "… know even less. But you think you do. Which makes you dangerous."

NINE

Night had passed slowly as Justyn traveled in and out of sleep.

The first few awakenings left him momentarily confused but now he'd made the mental shift to everything being upside-down. The thin fabric of the former ceiling cab was all he had so he made the best of it. The seats and dashboard were useless, made for the opposite orientation. It was cramped. Would have been in any situation. But the fall had dented it inward and now there was a spot about two feet square, close to the passenger side, flat enough to lay down in. Movement was restricted. Knees touched chest, necessary for both his physical circumstances and body heat. The lone intruder to his new abode was a tree limb, about six inches in circumference. It had wedged in between some side panel material and was hollow, or mostly so. It whistled quietly now and then, signaling the fortuitous inflow of air. Justyn imagined it would carry carbon dioxide the same way. At least he hoped so.

It was dark but not black.

He exhaled and his breath hung for just a second.

Justyn was glad he had brought the winter jacket. That was a last-minute catch. He'd laid it on a workbench in the storage unit where the van was parked. Prep kept him preoccupied. His phone buzzed. An email from Richards.

Get on the road. Now.

He grabbed his backpack and stepped into the cab. Starting her up, he eyed the workspace and the coat through the large, clear windshield.

Oh, man. Need that. Omaha's gonna be nasty.

The parka was helping everywhere it could but he was out of luck above the shoulders. Justyn had fought the idea of a knit cap. No matter how his contacts had warned him. It was totally a vanity move. Didn't want to mess up his hair.

Well, his hair was fine.

But he knew that inside his body bad things were happening.

His cough was worsening. A hoarseness more than just from the cold, although his nose was running and eyes watering as well. He'd spit up a small amount of blood earlier, but none in the last few hours. For sure, he had some ribcage issues. Broken or just bruised badly, didn't matter. He winced with every move of his torso. Good thing he couldn't do much of that.

Two times during the night he had tried to open the doors. Even if he had been able to position himself correctly, the pressure from the snow was an immovable force. And breaking the glass would only expose him further to the cold. On his own, there was no way out.

A slight shiver worked its way through his body. Small convulsions led to one big one.

"Ahgggg." He shook and his elbow hit what remained of the glove compartment.

A small pouch fell. The malshaped plastic and metal had held something back during the crash. A tire pressure gauge and folded papers had fallen from the initial impact. This must have gotten stuck.

Justyn's eyes widened.

The personal heating pack nearly glowed in his mind.

Surely, this was a sign. One among many.

Another moment of clarity. Another moment leading him here surfaced. Five years had passed but the experience was much the same.

"That's about right."

The small circle of teens backed away from the locker. Heinous painted words soiled the hallway. So out of place. School dance posters. Basketball rally ribbons. Everything else spoke of reasonably innocent adolescence. This was something entirely other. The kind of ugliness ingrained over more advanced seasons of life.

"Ha. Teach them something."

High fives as they walked away.

The boys were lifelong friends, natives of the small town, woven into its very fabric. Outside observers would have a hard time squaring their social standing with what they'd just done. Not everyone in town carried this worldview. Mostly a few, important clans. Justyn's father would have been uncomfortable with his recent trajectory and associations. His mom was doing the best she knew how. Recently widowed, she was just trying to hold it all together. With three kids and the sorrow of losing her husband to cancer, she felt pretty good about getting food on the table most days.

Justyn gravitated into their orbit, just the same. He was welcomed, if not fully baptized. One degree of social distance aggravated his own deep hurts and made the young man strive— and long—for even more. He'd figured out the relational calculus, seizing every opportunity to move up and in.

Early that evening, Justyn hovered near his friend's opened car hood. While the '65 Mustang was in near-mint exterior condition, the birthday present of a year ago needed a little care on the inside. They both watched in awe as an older man performed seeming magic on the engine.

"So," his friend's uncle started, looking around and then out the garage doorway. "Heard you boys made a statement."

Neither knew if they should speak.

"It's okay," the uncle stood back, wiping grease away. "We know. We keep an eye out."

"Uh," Justyn's friend stammered. "Thanks…"

"No problem. You know, we're all family, right? Even you, Justyn. Family. And family has each other's backs. Because we're not all family. But you know who you are, right boys? And you know who they are. *What* they are. I'm proud of you for standing up for what's yours. Justyn?"

The teen leaned in.

"You're the best point guard we got. That's what I hear."

Justyn beamed.

"So," he paused. "You gotta take what's yours. No right for anybody to just walk in and claim it. That coach of yours. Maybe he means well. Have to imagine some pressure there to even things out."

"We blacked out the camera," the nephew offered, seeing the conversation as safe.

"Yeah?" the uncle replied. "Stayed out of view?"

"Yep. Came up from behind and sprayed it. After practice. Everyone was gone already."

"Well," the man offered. "Not everybody."

The boys looked alarmed.

"And that sweatshirt is pretty bright. Probably show up on a camera, even as a hand comes around to block it out."

They understood. Be careful, yes. But they had others on their side.

"Not bad. Life skills, boys. Some things you'll only get better at with time. But not bad."

Justyn seethed. "I am not riding the bench. This whole thing is just so ridiculous. So unfair. I've worked my tail off, every year. And they just think they can move in, take over. *No*. What's mine is mine."

"You're right, Justyn. I've seen you play," the uncle fueled. "And I can't stand the thought of our team losing just because some beaurocrat thinks we need some kind of equal representation. What kind of world is that, where we don't let the best do their thing. You know what? Even if he was better than you, which is clearly not the case, it's our town. Our school. Our team. There's other places they should be. No, I'm proud of you boys. Did the right thing today. The sooner they understand they belong elsewhere, the better it'll be. For everyone."

The boys turned to the call for dinner. They were famished and Justyn knew the offerings at home would be far more meager.

That night Justyn replayed the day, in bed, drifting off. He couldn't express it as fully as he'd like but a demarcation was growing in his mind and heart. Us. Them. Life as a zero-sum game. No, not a game. A battle. And battles call for soldiering.

"I am a warrior."

The practiced mantra flowed with conviction over even breaths, levitating in the cold, upturned van.

"My battle is just. *The Family*, my band of brothers."

Justyn shook the pouch. It began to radiate heat and warmth for his body. Even as the memories warmed his soul.

TEN

"Hello?"

Carter caught the greeting and pulled up from his paperwork, glancing at the parked cruiser's dashboard clock. *Yikes. 11:15?*

A man stood a few feet away, arms spread in mock surrender, steaming cup in his right hand.

The trooper powered down the passenger side window.

"Officer?"

"Sir," Carter replied. "Something I can help with?"

"Oh, no. Just thankful you're doing what you're doing and thought I'd bring you some coffee. Guessed on the blend. Seen you here a few times in our parking lot and meant to connect the next time."

Carter's gaze trailed past him.

Church at the Heights.

He remembered noticing the sign the first time but it had become such a routine spot it no longer registered. The man was about his age, slightly balding. Threat level: zero. Police work had made him more aware, but not completely jaded.

"Sure. Ah, Pastor?"

"Sam. You can just call me Sam. But yeah, if you want someone to blame around here," he joked, handing over the cup.

Carter felt the unintentional barb but decided he'd bury it with a quick sip of the liquid offering.

"Wow."

"I thought you'd like it. Honduran. Just got it in last week from some friends. You know," Sam continued, "You can stop into the cafe anytime. Always on the house for other folks trying to do good things in our community."

Carter wanted to not like the guy. From only a few moments of interaction, he seemed, what—happy?—at his church. Completely illogically, that made him grumpy. But the coffee was *so* good. And what's with the cafe? A cafe? His former elders had made him use the nasty grounds they bought two or three times before throwing them out. Church coffee in Carter's old world had been universally horrid. His new world at District 3 wasn't an improvement by any stretch. So, this was weird. Weird, but still worth finishing. And he needed it. The last few minutes he was admittedly fading.

The day had started early. The HomeSec briefing and the argument with Bradford. Always, Bradford. What was her problem, anyway? If she knew anything, anything at all about him, she'd ease up. Her assumptions were way out of line. At least, from his vantage point. Sometimes it felt like he'd traded one set of assailants for another. He had no stomach for unending workplace battles. It ate at him nearly every shift.

And then there was that goofy van plate thing.

"So, like I said," Sam finished. "Just really appreciate all you do. On my way out for lunch super quick. If you're here for a bit, can I bring you something?"

Over the top.

Sure, back in the day he would likely have done the same thing. But, still.

"Oh, no. I mean, that's nice. But I am on my way in just a minute." Carter displayed a plastic-wrapped ham sandwich. "Got it covered."

Sam held his hands up again. Such a funny, universal gesture.

"Thanks, Pastor... uh, Sam."

Sam held out a piece of paper. "You have kids? They'll love it. Kinda late notice but tomorrow being a teacher workday, we try to help."

WinterFest. Thursday 9am-3pm.

Games. Inflatables. Archery tag. Crafts. Lunch and hot drinks.

Carter was even more jealous. He also knew Theo and Mia would love it. And Mae could use the coverage. She worked from home and a school day off was always a challenge. Plus, when was the last time he'd been able to take in something like this with his kids? Too long. First year with the badge meant he was always on call. Though well-intended, union rules were more like guidelines. He wanted to become a good cop. He also very much wanted to be a great dad.

And archery tag? Maybe they'd let him play if he promised to go easy.

He took the flyer as non-committaly as possible.

Sam closed the sale. "See you tomorrow... uh, hadn't caught your name yet. "

"Jons. Carter Jons. Looks like a lot of fun. Not sure we can make it... but thanks."

Sam waved.

The trooper slid the window back up, knowing that last part was a complete lie. He was off tomorrow and already planning on being there with his kids. He was also really, really wanting a reason to stay away.

The next couple hours passed as routinely as the paperwork stop at the church parking lot. But these hours were spent on the road.

Posted at the junction of 29 and 680, Carter watched drivers perform roughly the same set of behaviors for about an hour. Approach at excessive speed. Catch a glimpse of his cruiser from a few hundred yards out. Manage a faster than natural deceleration. Hit close to posted speed right before they came up on him and then prayer. Lots of prayer.

5 MPH was the unofficial buffer. Everyone knew the rules. Not everyone used them wisely. This time of year many drivers still didn't believe they could lose control. Didn't matter that everything was white, all around. If the pavement was reasonably clear they assumed all was good.

His Dodge Charger could hit 60 in 6 seconds and top out at over a hundred-fifty. While that meant he could chase most vehicles down with ease, it didn't mean anything if the accident had already happened. Except he might be able to get there a few seconds earlier, and that could be a blessing or a curse, depending on what he found on approach.

Carter hadn't seen the worst of it yet. District 3 had its stories. A few too gruesome to focus on for long. Earlier this year he'd been called to an accident scene where sorrowful tragedy had been graciously averted. He remembered looking at the depleted airbags in wonder and thinking a few angels got pretty banged up that afternoon placing themselves between the four grade-school-aged kids and shards of metal and glass.

They'd all just walked away. For sure, they weren't shaken. But they walked away nonetheless.

Carter's training helped him assess and respond. All was meant to be clinical, orderly. Facts. Evidence. Reporting. Still, it was near-impossible to not imagine Mae and the kids in that car. His heart sank, even as he checked out skid patterns and distances.

For some odd reason, the image striking deepest was the tow truck pulling the car up onto its platform and driving away, hazard lights silently flashing. It all looked so final. So weak. Lifeless. That could have been the story for that family, that day, as well.

Carter nearly mashed the radio handset.

"District 3 Dispatch. Jons here."

"3 Dispatch, 10-4."

"I need some images pulled from 80 between Des Moines and that Loves Travel Stop at Shelby. The white van."

The shift sergeant was nearby, overheard, and stepped in.

"Jons?"

"Sarge? Yeah. We need somebody on those images. Immediately."

"Images. I thought we didn't have any images before Shelby and that was the problem."

"Sir, correct. We don't. At least not any Ford Transits on the road."

"You're not making any sense at all, Jons. What? You want us to look for an old white cargo van... *not* on the road?"

"Sort of. I think it may not have gotten to Shelby on its own power. I think it may have been towed. We've been looking for that car, out on the road, not on a rack. What if whoever didn't want it seen just used some subtle camouflage? I mean, a vehicle being towed is not operable, right? I don't remember seeing our vehicle on a rack in any of the other images. But honestly, that's not what I was looking for."

"Alright. Strange, but probably worth an hour of someone's time here. You can jump in when you get back. I'll get Bradford on it."

Seriously? Bradford?

"Sir. Uh… "

"What? Something else, Jons?"

"No. Nothing, sir."

"Good. Get back to District asap. 3 out."

ELEVEN

West Kansas looked a lot like East Colorado.

Townsend kept his gaze on the pavement. The earlier events of the day played at the edges of his thinking. Not quite drowned out by purpose. Or the radio talk show host's barking.

"So there you have it, my friends. An administration that is hell-bent on the destruction of our identity. They have no respect, no value for what we've been handed. The Framers are not just rolling over in their graves. They're spinning. And if they could come back, they'd smack us upside the head and demand to know why we're so very stupid."

Townsend nodded.

"But you know, we deserve this. It's our own inability at the ballot box that keeps us in this perpetual state of decline. And you know that's the plan, right? No one agrees to replace a system that's working. Prosperous, free people don't start revolutions. But just make things worse, little by little. Then we all wake up one day to see that our government and very lives are no longer recognizable."

Perry's grip tightened. His jaw clenched.

"And what is the one lever they keep pulling? Over and over again? What is the wedge they keep forcing into place?"

A pause.

"Group identity. That's it. That simple. Maximize our differences and minimize our commonalities. Could be race. Could be religion. Anything that can get me looking at *you* suspiciously. Anything that can keep *us* from being one America."

Townsend frowned, reaching for the radio.

"You had me. And then you lost me," he proclaimed. "Couldn't be more wrong. There is one America. Just not the kind you're thinking."

The engine knocking came on suddenly.

What?

Townsend checked his mirrors. Then he signaled and pulled into the right-hand lane. The road wasn't empty but neither was it rush hour outside a major city. He could get over to the gravel and check it out if needed.

"Ah, c'mon," he growled, searching the front hood and then back in his mirrors. No smoke. Still, he had plenty more road in front of him to just hope it would be okay.

This was not part of the plan.

Perry let it bang for another few seconds. It only became more insistent.

A small rest stop appeared and he headed for the offramp.

Ogallah, Kansas. Population 28.

The tiny stop had four parking spaces, all marked for the size of a compact. He decided to take the last two. Hopping out, he opened the hood, looking for an obvious problem and an equally obvious solution.

The engine was running, heat radiating. Still, the weather's cold struck his hands within seconds. His face scrunched up, eyes searching for who knew what. Townsend was not a mechanic.

Wasn't even mechanically inclined. He'd tried a few times but it wasn't his thing.

Ping. Ping.

Nothing looked loose from where he stood.

Townsend took a step back to the cab and shut the engine off.

Then he felt it. The last few hours of coffee.

The rest area was as basic as could be. One forlorn picnic table and an overflowing garbage can. A single standard issue porta-potty. No trees. It would be more obvious if he relieved himself out in the open.

He stepped quickly over and into the plastic and aluminum john and closed the door. Inside was slightly warmer but the smell was horrendous. Traffic buzzed by on I70, creating an odd resonance. He finished. Then he heard the sound of tires pulling to a stop outside. Townsend exited to the sight of a middle-aged man leaning into his van's engine compartment.

"Hey," he approached slowly.

"Oh hey," the man stood up. "You got trouble? Thought I'd take a look for ya."

"Well, uh. Yeah, you really don't need to do that."

"What was it? Didn't see anything in there that looked too bad. I mean, a little rust here and there. To be expected for a truck this old."

Townsend's face gave away the truth, but he lied nonetheless. "Yeah, no. I'm good."

A thin metallic clink pulled both of them in.

The man was under the front of the car far more quickly than Townsend would have imagined.

"Ah, yeah. There she is."

In only another few seconds he was back upright, holding a circular piece of metal with a small yet significant break.

"Ha. Was gonna happen sooner or later. You're lucky it was near here. Clamp for the exhaust hose coming off. That falls and drags, maybe you get a spark. Nice little flare-up, most likely."

Townsend breathed, thinking of his cargo.

You have no idea.

"I got some duct tape and gorilla glue."

Of course, you do.

Townsend was stuck. He needed the simple repair. He likely would never have found it on his own. Also, no, he didn't have duct tape or gorilla glue.

And now he had no choice.

The second time wasn't any easier.

Heading steadily east he needed to focus, just get back on track and get to his meet-up. The clock was ticking, evermore toward their target and their schedule.

Townsend turned the radio back on.

"Look. You have to listen to me very, very carefully," the show host continued. "It's not enough to just stand by anymore. This is a time for action. Where are the ones courageous enough to do what is necessary? Do you *hear* me, America? If we don't step up, we will be the end of the line. The country that has been the promise of the world... God's idea... we won't be able to hand it off to our children, or their children."

Townsend's eyes narrowed. His heart pounded.

"We are the last line of defense. We are the ones who will look back on our lives in thankfulness or remorse."

He drove on, body rigid.

"Prepare. Prepare now," the host's tone shifted. "And we want you to have the very best in preparedness resourcing. That's why *My Patriot Depot* is your number one choice for nonperishable, ready-to-cook meals and … "

Townsend thrust his finger into the power button.

You're the one who has no idea what's coming. You're only making things worse. You're a fraud. You're no patriot. Patriots do the hard things. You're just selling products.

He drove on, working very hard to leave the tragic stop behind.

It had taken another half hour — time he did not have — to drive the man's car to a reasonable hiding place. The walk back through fallow fields was so cold. But the distance would be worth it. By the time he was reported missing and enough clues led back, Townsend would be multiple hundreds of miles away.

The man didn't deserve this kind of end.

But Townsend's mission couldn't allow for that kind of thinking.

TWELVE

Richards liked the bird's eye view even better.

The Hilton Omaha had rooftop parking. Her architects thought of space, efficiency, capacity, and overall aesthetic — out of view from ground level. Richards appreciated the latter while ignoring the former. More importantly, the view from here was a perfect compliment to his research on foot.

The eight-story structure gave him eyes on to the arena's outer layers. Much of CHI Health Center's road-facing exterior was glass. From his parking space, the grand entrance was in full view as were the ramps heading to each level of the structure. He could not see into the field house interior but that didn't matter. His work wasn't a show. There was no message he desired to express from mid-field or, in this case, the massive stage and dais.

No. The building's engineering was his focus.

He knew where the concrete and steel would buckle. This was, in fact, his expertise, apparently not found among his employer's minions. Makes sense. They were all stupid zealots anyways. Driven by their cause. When would they have the time, or the smarts, to study physics or chemistry? It's a wonder they all hadn't blown themselves to kingdom come already. He didn't care, one way or another. He wasn't going to be a martyr for anyone. Just another paycheck.

Richards made a few more mental notes, internal calculations. They were on track. Especially now that he'd learned he'd have the other half of the materials to work with.

Two, simple, easily obtainable substances. Not the usual suspects. State and federal law enforcement had made that almost impossible since Oklahoma City. Supplies of that particular fertilizer and diesel were more and more scrutinized. Richards' personal advancement in the field was the destructive effect of a less likely home-repair compound and biofuel.

He smirked.

Stupid Greens. Just as bad as these other guys. Beliefs before all else. Think they're saving the world. Just giving me more things to go boom.

The hired gun had everything he needed to make a dent and then half of what he needed for complete devastation. Justyn's replacement was on the way with the rest.

What had happened to the young punk?

He didn't care. As long as it didn't jeopardize his work. He'd only met him once. Thought he was an idiot, then, too.

The meeting took place, unexpectedly, in the rather well-appointed living room of a suburban home.

Richards rarely met his employers. He had hedged on this one, too. But they'd given him options. One: just show up and do the job himself. Meet no one. Digital transfer of payment. That was pretty standard and the best way to have an actual career in this line of work. Two: meet once. A partner from their ranks. Quadruple the money. They knew their target, he'd reflected. Could do a little damage with little risk or a whole lot more with a bit more exposure. They were willing to chance it. For the money, so was he.

Before agreeing, they insisted he meet Justyn. The young man walked into the room. He carried himself well. Probably an athlete. But fervor filled his eyes and Richards was always wary of the believers. Justyn had mentioned *The Family* more than once in their brief two minutes of conversation. That creeped Richards out even more.

"You can guarantee it?" the host leaned in.

"Care to be more specific?" Richards offered.

The man was wary. No, he was full-on paranoid.

Richards met him halfway. "Yeah, *tens.*"

The host's eyes widened. "Okay, then. Looks like you're our man."

Richards knew he was anything but.

Arrangements for a deposit and then the subsequent five months of planning followed. Both men wanted success, even with very different motivations.

Justyn was reeling at the euphemism. He kept his mouth shut but it was a challenge.

Tens. Ten. Ten *thousand* casualties. They'd strike a blow deeper than anyone. Ever. Bigger than Pearl Harbor. Bigger than 9/11. And those had been the enemies of America. They were going to save her. Anyone still on the sidelines would rush to the cause of rightness. The political and social cabal that had held his nation in check for so long was about to be weakened, maybe beyond repair. Or maybe they would foolishly counter. That was fine, too. His heart beat faster at the thought of it all. This would be the turning point. The fulcrum.

Revival.

Richards saw it all play out on Justyn's face and nearly called it off, right there. He didn't need passion. He needed proficiency. Professionalism. Good luck finding that among such fanaticism. In the end, cash won him over. He wouldn't need many more jobs like this if he indeed wanted at some point to call it quits.

10th Street had a single traffic light out front of the arena.

Richards' eyes followed north and south. Either path would provide a clean exfil. Didn't matter because he would be long gone when the timers ran down. He would head east and disappear. Still, he needed confirmation of a job well done. A visual invoice of sorts.

Stepping out of his sedan he walked over to the edge of the building. He pulled out a slim oval no larger than a quarter and placed it onto the outside edge of the guardrail, pointing directly at CHI Health. Back inside the car he pulled up his specialized camera app, chose the correct source, and then set it for day after tomorrow, 7:20pm CST. There would be no disagreement on payment. And he did like to see the quality of his work.

Once out of the building, he turned the car left, heading back to his hotel.

His phone screen woke.

Better half on the way. Late tonight.

Richards grimaced. Amateurs. Posing as something far more important. But in the end, amateurs. He carried the slightest doubt about pairing up with them. Those concerns vanished with the thought of eight figures as he passed his hotel, knowing now he had a little less time than presumed.

Parking streetside, north of the city, Richards walked the last hundred yards.

He waited for the attendant to be distracted by another customer. Picking up the pace, he got past unnoticed and strolled down the long line of orange and white units. Three digits got him in and he pulled the garage door shut. Inside, he flicked the overhead lights on.

The white cargo van sat quiet and cold.

But its contents were primed for terror and death.

THIRTEEN

"Hey. Do your own work next time, rookie."

Carter turned toward the open bay in District 3's garage. The massive double overhead door settled closed with a pneumatic hiss.

"What?"

Bradford took another step toward Carter's cruiser, stopping at the front left bumper.

"I said do your own work next time, Jons. Everyone is busy around here. No special favors for the newb."

"Okay…" he processed the suddenly serious conversation.

"Got it?"

"Look, Bradford. Sorry you got pulled into it. Just thought we needed to press that search forward and I was still out on the pavement."

"It was stupid."

"Huh?"

"You don't think someone would have noticed? We're looking for a particular white van. Okay, nowhere on the road before the travel stop and then we get a plate change further west. That's enough to peak interest. Enough for good troopers to be looking for other options."

"Like a tow."

"Like a tow. So, yeah, huge waste of time. For me. And anyone else given the ridiculous task."

"I guess it came up negative, then."

"Now you're doing some fine police work there, Jons."

"Bradford. Sorry, again," he paused "that you got pulled in. Had a theory. Wanted it checked out. You know, with all that's going on."

"What? Now you believe the HomeSec alerts? You *are* a piece of work, Jons."

"Care to elaborate?"

"This morning? Seems like data only matters when it suits your 'theories.' You do know what that's called, right?"

"Okay, I'll bite. Hit me with the speech about bias confirmation, please. Because to me, it seems you're riding that line pretty heavily on your own."

Bradford moved a step closer.

Carter stayed put.

"I owe you nothing. Nothing. If you were just an ordinary guy, I'd pass you off without a second thought. Your ignorance is none of my business. And eventually, you'd fold under the weight of it. Problem is, you're not just anybody. You're a sworn peace officer of the State of Iowa. And no, this isn't Alabama. But that doesn't mean all is well. We have real problems and you don't seem to want to acknowledge that."

"Whoah. Hang on. I am very concerned. Obviously. You know the job. You know the pay scale. If I didn't think law and order was a foundational issue in our community, the community my family lives in by the way, why would I be doing this?"

"I have no doubt you're concerned with law and order. It's just whose laws and what kind of order."

Carter opened his mouth. And then shut it again.

He moved past her and into the hallway.

"Thanks for the help on the search."

His heavy coat and hat came off and then onto the wall hooks in frustration.

She was right.

Carter was so convinced they'd find the white van in some form of tow. He'd spent the better part of an hour going over her work. Nothing. Just like she said.

He walked over to the shift sergeant's small, enclosed space. Barely a closet. Clear panels, just enough to fit a small desk. He knocked.

"Jons."

"Sarge. Got a second?"

"I do. I'd offer you a seat, but," he motioned "well, that's just not possible."

"Yeah. Standing is fine."

"Good."

"So, that tow search."

"Empty, I heard."

"Ah, yeah. Checked it out again myself."

"Happens. Sometimes ideas don't pan out."

"So, I'd like to widen the radius. And maybe even get a couple other districts on it?"

The superior officer looked up fully now.

"Jons. That's not gonna happen."

"Which? I mean I'd be glad to run the images myself here and I know it's an ask, but the other shops might want to know what we found."

"Which is what, again?"

"I mean, we can't just let this go, right?"

"Trooper Jons," he upped the ante. "Force strength is down. It's winter. Unless you haven't noticed. We've got our hands full already."

"I've got another two hours before end of shift."

"No."

Carter stopped, weighing his next words.

"Sir," he slowed. "What about a CAB?"

The sergeant considered it. A Community Awareness Bulletin wasn't more work than a simple email. Neither was it a perfect net as interested businesses, community entities, and individuals had to opt into the notifications. But it was a fairly wide net. A see-something-say-something kind of tool.

"Fine," he relented. "Type it up. Get it to me. I'll review it and send it."

Carter turned to leave.

"Jons."

"Sir."

"You and Bradford."

"Yes."

"Good thing we're not local police. You two wouldn't exactly be partner of the year candidates. Look, you don't need to be best friends. But you do need to respect one another. Enough to trust each other when it counts."

"Yes, sir. I mean, yeah she's not easy to get along with. But her work is definitely worthy of that."

"Okay, but is *she* worthy of that? You know she's a person, right?"

The words struck hard. Carter chided himself. Of course, she was a person. Made in God's image, just like him. Fallen, yes. Just like him. Complex? Certainly. Wasn't that the case with all six billion of us? She'd just been so infuriating. Why in the world did she need to come after him all the time? He was doing good work, too.

"Jons?"

"Sir. Yes, absolutely. We'll figure it out."

The older man wasn't completely convinced.

"See that you do."

At his desk, Carter's phone screen flashed.

The image opened along with the text message.

Theo's art skills were at that age where the human form was not quite perfected, yet wonderfully playful. Head to torso ratio was like 3 to 1. Arms protruded where ears should be. Eyes comically wide open. Chicken legs.

Carter pushed the phone call icon. It rang.

"Hey, babe," Mae answered.

"Ha. Hey sweetie. You have no idea how much I needed that."

"Oh, another rough one? We were just having some afternoon craft time and he wanted to send you a picture."

"Well, it was perfect timing. I love you guys."

"Off soon?"

"Yeah. Just need to wrap up a few things here. By the way, and I am not a professionally trained therapist, but Theo's drawing seems quite intuitive."

"Is that right?"

"Yup. But it has me a little concerned that he's making you look so grumpy. I mean, look at that hair. And the angle of your head?"

"Carter."

"Yeah?"

"That's you. Not me."

Silence.

"Well," he floundered. "Have I been that bad, lately?"

"Maybe?" she offered softly. "No blame. You've got a few reasons. But the kids. They know you love them. They just want a little more happy and a little less grumpster. Maybe that church fun day tomorrow? Still on your radar?"

Radar. Bulletin.

"Yes, my dear. But it's only because they have good coffee. Which reminds me. I was hoping to stop by that new coffee shop on the way home for a bit. A little reading maybe before dinner? Bring you some dark roast? Beans or ground?"

"Beans. Sounds great, Carter. 6pm, though. Dinner will be ready."

"I seriously don't deserve you."

"You're correct on that one, trooper."

The phone clicked off and Carter turned his attention to the keyboard.

Community Awareness Bulletin. Wed 4:45pm.

District 3 of the Iowa State Patrol has issued a notice regarding an early 2000s model Ford Transit Van…

FOURTEEN

Justyn could sense it.

The *Family* was supporting him, even from a distance. He knew it. And he needed it.

Since finding the warming pack earlier in the morning he'd kept it near his neck. Eight of its ten hours of usefulness had passed as Justyn's first twenty-four of entrapment ended. Providentially, another one had also loosened and fallen from the back of the glove compartment.

Newly encouraged, the young man gathered his meager belongings and began to organize himself for survival. His backpack held a pencil and a notebook. He liked to sketch. Had found some success artistically but never followed up in any formal manner. The pages were filled with his attempts to embody the teachings he had been entrusted.

Page 43. The wolf was impressive. Eyes ablaze. Bared teeth. Muscle and sinew poised for action. Details of fur, claw, and tail all flowing from the monochrome tip of an ordinary number 2 pencil. It wasn't clinical accuracy. More metaphor. Ready to do its duty. Standing guard, willing and able. At the bottom edge of the page lay two smaller animals. Cowering. Lesser. Weaker. This was the order of the natural world.

"The meek shall inherit the earth. But someone must rule over the meek."

The hand lettering spoke volumes.

Beside the notebook a water bottle, small flashlight, and multitool completed his kit. Justyn's phone and extra charging pack were the only other items in his little trove. The screen had been badly damaged but he could still see that the battery was waning down. Seventeen percent. Its faint glow had been another encouragement, besides the warming pouches, even if no signal was present.

For this, Justyn had cursed the area's rural simpletons more than once, longing for just a bar or two to appear.

Flippin' twenty-first century. A few more cell towers wouldn't hurt. Idiots.

He reached over and powered down the phone. Give it a few hours. Maybe it's just a storm. He couldn't tell from under all this snow.

Extending his arm hurt. Bad.

Justyn winced. Then he coughed. Red flecks landed on the ceiling—his floor. He coughed again, this time losing control. His head snapped forward, neck straining. His chest burned with pain. Licking his lips and spitting out more red. He felt deep cracks forming, likely the source of at least some of the blood. Maybe internal wasn't as bad after all.

The headache, though, pressed mercilessly.

He'd done his best to ration the last third of the liquid in his stainless steel canister. A little during the night. A little more this morning. But there wasn't much to begin with. Now, it was empty. And the growing pain in his head was at least partly due to dehydration.

Like everything else among his meager resources, it was all a matter of timing. A significant water supply lay all around him. But that would require breaching the glass, removing the thin protective veil and inviting even more cold into his world. If he wanted any kind of volume, he'd need to melt the snow as well. Which meant it would need to be during a heat pouch's lifespan. The equation had a few, simple variables. He just wasn't quite sure yet when to put the pieces into play. These items were finite. Time was the unknown.

He could deal with the pain for now.

Justyn reached into his backpack.

More pain as he extracted the journal and pencil.

He kept his right arm close to his side. It helped some but made his strokes awkward.

A few basic verticals, although at an odd angle. Four ovals, somewhat evenly spaced. More lines. Some shading.

The upturned van appeared on the page.

The chosen will rise.

Justyn finished the lettering and laid the book aside, page open to draw strength from its truth. He forced himself to recall the first time he'd heard that promise.

The ceremony was brief. It was also life-changing.

He remembered everything about it. It was in a church. Not his family's church. But that was irrelevant. They'd stopped attending regularly more than a few years back. Justyn looked around. Five adults in their forties. Three candidates, himself included. Candles on a stand. Was that an old scouting bridge? Yeah, it was. He'd stepped across one like it when he was ten years old. He took an oath then. He was taking one now.

The building itself made certain truth claims. Stained glass and fabrics. Banners. The words invoked by the first adult were a mix of these, albeit more generalized spiritually with significant additions of nation and tribe. It was heady. His very soul was afire with the call, the charge to protect, to assure primacy, to ensure legacy.

Would he, at all costs, and at all times, bind himself to these dictums, to his people, to this family? Would he take his place in *The Family*?

Justyn's eyes glazed, sweeping across the flickering firelight. All else dimmed in the room. That was the point. Darkness. Light. Who wouldn't want to be filled with light? Why wouldn't you fight a growing darkness?

He repeated their words, slowly, meaningfully. Then he took seven steps, the number stipulated by his elders, and crossed over.

At nineteen, Justyn had pledged himself to an entirely new life.

Across the small bridge and on his knees, another elder passed a Bible over his head. A third elder, to this point silent, gazed at the three initiates. Then he spoke the words of certainty.

Justyn took them in again, breathing deeply even through pain, holding them as true today as he did then.

The chosen will rise.

His circumstances were not his destiny.

Lazarus rose. Jesus rose. The white surrounding him was simply a test. A call to righteousness. He need only show strength. Valor. Loyalty. It could not end this way. They'd assured him of it. But... what if this wasn't a test? What if this was his fault? What if he had been the one to fail *The Family*? Had he been operationally diligent to pull off the interstate when he did? Or was he just scared?

The weather had all but shut down traffic. State and local police, everywhere. He couldn't get stopped. What if they found some reason to inspect his load? He'd wandered along the side roads, looking for a way back. More snow. Visibility near-zero. A flash of headlights. Was that red and blue on top of the car? The Iowa State Trooper Seal in a blur?

Justyn swerved. Thirty more feet and he saw the road curve. Or at least he thought he did. Another hundred feet and he knew he'd made an error. Every choice after that only pulled him further into the snow. Then trees. And more snow. Sliding to the very edge of the small farm bridge, hanging precariously. Forward, Reverse. Rocking the van. He leaned with every effort, as if his body weight could make the difference, freeing his wildly spinning wheels. The last shift dug deeper on the back left. The entire van leaned back and over. Justyn reached for the door, fingers barely touching the handle. There was no stopping it now.

The roll and the drop.

Head against windshield.

Justyn remembered.

And for the briefest moment, Justyn doubted.

FIFTEEN

The carton of eggs made the expected mess on the aging linoleum.

"Oh, you've got to be kidding me." The older proprietor looked around the small space. "Judy?"

He looked away from the counter again.

"Ju…"

"What's all the yappin' for?"

It was Judy.

Don had his hands in exasperation mode.

"Can you get that cleaned up, Judy? I got a full line here and three more pumps coming in to pay."

"Well, I guess," Judy walked over.

The customer was still red. Asked if they could just get some paper towels or something. Glad to pay for them. Really, really sorry.

Judy waved them off. "No, no. That's not how we do things around here. You get another carton. I got this." She brightened with the task. "Clean up on aisle three!"

Don rolled his eyes.

There were only three aisles, each a sum total of five feet long, in the Quick Stop at McClelland, Iowa.

Judy got to work, even whistled a little, and had it all cleaned up in about thirty seconds. Her attention to the matter spoke pride of service. And ownership. She and Don had operated this little slice of local economy and culture since 1982.

Everyone knew Don and, especially everyone knew Judy.

The Quick Stop wasn't just gas, milk, and cigs. Somehow, amazingly, they always had what you needed. Everything. Maybe only one of whatever it was you needed but then again they restocked items almost magically. This couple took their role in this small town seriously. It was the only option for fuel and only other option, besides the GrocerMart, for food. Most others in their situation would take advantage of market forces and up-charge everything. Not these two. Same prices as the bigger store and always five cents cheaper on gas than surrounding towns. Don had farmed most of his life. Knew the razor-thin margins. No, the Quick Stop was a part of McClelland, here for good, both literally and figuratively.

"Don, you and Judy are the best," remarked the man first in line.

"Well, we're just glad to be here, Bill. Now, how is your Bess?"

"She's fightin'. Real hard."

Don knew the chemo was taking its toll. It's a strange world when you poison in order to heal.

"Well, that's good. Real good. We're praying, me and Judy."

Bill knew it was true. More than a way to close an uncomfortable conversation. He'd bet they were on their knees every night, banging on heaven's doors for his wife of forty-three years.

He'd be right.

The crowd eventually cleared out.

"Not a bad afternoon. Not bad at all. Judy, hon?"

She stopped stocking items.

"You want backroom today?"

"What?" she offered. "Miss out on all the scuttlebut? In the next half hour Miss Petersen will come looking for her pre-supper sweetroll. She's always got a story or two."

"Fair enough. But you know what the good book says about gossip, right?"

"Why, Donald Baxter. It's not gossip… if it's true."

He smiled, shook his head lightly, and walked back to the office.

He'd pulled the cash from the drawer and was running the credit transactions as well. A good afternoon, it was. The Baxters used a mix of paper and electronic systems. A few modernizations had seemed helpful to adopt, but they at heart were old-school business owners. They knew enough to keep things running. They knew enough to enjoy their work. While Don was usually the one to count receipts, Judy was definitely in charge of supply. Even the fuel contracts. In year two of their venture she'd chewed out an oil rep for pricing sleight of hand and questionable practices. That had been the first and the last of such encounters.

Don got the numbers in reasonable order and turned his attention to a multi-screen just left of his desk. The setup seemed way too techy for them, installed after the only robbery they'd ever experienced. Turned out to be one of the Palmer kids. They weren't bad, just need some direction. A nephew, Judy's sister's son, had priced out the cameras, computer, and monthly service and online storage fees. The older couple was fine with the first two but absolutely would not pay for the third. Why? Doesn't the computer have storage already? Their nephew tried to explain it. Something about frame rates, resolution, or whatever.

The Baxters were at their little store most of the daylight hours of every day. They had two part-time attendants covering the evening. Don's routine with the video only required him to review the overnight, when they were closed. And it was super handy that he could run it at ten times speed. Ten pm to five am. 7 hours. 420 minutes. 42 at speed.

Don pulled up the video file. He'd check the first few minutes — just to make sure the file was good — and then fast-forward to the parts he was not around. It had only advanced a minute when he clicked the mouse, pausing and then leaning in to read off the screen.

"Judy?" he scooted his chair out and into the tiny hallway leading upfront.

"Not now, Don. Miss Peterson's just arrived."

"Hey, Judy," he tried again.

"Can't it wait?"

He ignored her. "Hear about a new store in town?"

"New store? No."

"Buckner. B-u-c-k-n-e-r?"

"I can spell, old man. No. No new store I know of."

"Alright, then." He wheeled back.

Don fast-forwarded, pushed play at 10x again, images zooming by, as he scratched the white van's company name onto a piece of scrap paper.

"Buckner Feed and Seed," he reflected. "Well, whatever. Old Jim's got the best stuff around anyways."

Thirty-nine minutes and two games of solitaire later, he pushed a red button: "delete."

Then Don moved his mouse cursor to the right, pressing a green button, initiating the next recording.

Judy appeared in the office doorway.

"What was that about some new store?"

"Oh, nothin' much."

"Well, Debbie's here for night shift, so we can head home. And boy, have I got something to tell you…"

SIXTEEN

The coffee was pretty good.

Seats, a bit close for his liking. Carter had been here for a little over forty-five minutes. Busier than anticipated at this hour, he took a seat along the back wall after ordering.

"Carter," the barista set the hot drink on the counter.

Jons was so used to people calling him sir, officer, or using his last name that he didn't immediately react.

"Uh, yeah," he finally got up. "Thanks. Thanks very much."

Nothing. She was working on three other drinks. Not being rude, just busy. It was a brand new store and not just another coffee conglomerate. They'd do well if they brought that always sought after combo of local and good. And reasonably priced.

Carter noted everyone in the room on his way back. He'd done it on the way in as well. This wasn't a new behavior. In his previous line of work, coffee shops were a great way to be present, be known, in the community. Even if he was mostly doing sermon prep or just some reading, it led to interesting connections more often than you'd imagine.

So, the behavior wasn't novel. The motivation was. He tried very hard to keep awareness and curiosity from becoming suspicion. He didn't want to become jaded in a second career, as well. Everyone knew law enforcement officers that immediately categorized each person they met as potential threats. No fun. And not the best public relations for a line of work suffering from repeated bad press the last few years. This was something he and Mae had gone over before his decision to apply. She, as always was correct. There would be an uphill battle to become the kind of helpful presence he imagined of an Iowa State Trooper. Not so unlike those in the ministry, who'd had their fair share of recent public shortcomings as well.

She'd looked at him with "really?" more than a couple times.

And then there was the danger. He had a family to consider. On the grand scale, not an exaggerated risk profile. Nothing like generations of men throughout history who would go to war, often and repeatedly. Still, in modernity, actuarial tables favored actuaries, not police.

He'd ordered a dark roast. For years he'd been a cream and sugar guy. The last six months he more often took it black. Wondered if he'd been missing out on the actual flavor of coffee. Only in the last few weeks had he been able to note differences between blends. As he sipped he looked up.

Two men. Heads down. Speaking softly and not to each other. An open, paperback book in front of each.

Carter sighed.

Meeting one on one was his absolute favorite part of pastoring. Most people would imagine the preaching, or maybe leading, if asked what they thought ministers enjoyed most about their work. No. This, right here was the best. Connecting personally with another believer. Pouring over the Scriptures together. Praying. Caring and knowing what was going on in their lives, in their souls. Not that he could fix any of the bad things. Or take any measure of credit for the good. No, he knew better than that. He knew himself. He knew his failings. He also knew God's goodness,

His promises, and His presence.

Carter's phone buzzed. Assuming it would be Mae, he swiped it awake.

The email header grabbed him. He opened it.

Thomas Beckins, Attorney at Law.

Mr. Carter Jons.

Please be informed that civil court proceedings regarding your Roth Funds have been positively resolved. In the manner of Friendship Bible Church v Jons, the court finds no statutory or contractual means by which these funds must be relinquished. Lacking evidence, the court urged FBC to drop its case and settle, which they have done. We would be glad to confer at greater length as helpful but are pleased with the court's actions and the outcome of our defense.

Sincerely…

Carter knew he should also be pleased.

But then again, his lawyer had not been publicly accused of moral failure.

"You what?"

Carter was incredulous. No, he was furious.

"This is insane!"

"Pastor Jons," the head elder replied. "We're going to need you to calm down. These are the facts as we have them."

"Facts? From whom? Where?"

"Now, you know these kinds of claims are very serious. And very personal."

"So, I have no opportunity to even hear from my accuser. That's not right and you know it."

"Pastor," another elder stepped in. "This is not a criminal claim. None of your constitutional rights are being impinged upon. But it is very troubling. And we would be setting aside duties as spiritual leaders of this flock were we not to pursue the truth. We have sworn statements."

"So, someone told you I have been having an affair with them."

"Yes, and we've not enjoyed the level of detail she has shared with us, but it does corroborate her claims. Are you denying her accounts? It would be so much better were you to just confess, Pastor."

Carter racked his brain. He'd been so careful. He'd never let himself be alone with anyone. He knew this was falsehood, but why? What possible motive could there be for these men to fabricate such farce. Sure, they didn't like him. Had just fired him. But this. This was too much for even them.

It hit him.

Community Reach Hope Center.

She'd been a part-time admin there but only for a few weeks. His interactions with her had always been in groups. She'd left, abruptly. In confidence the minister at First Methodist shared her history and that she'd voluntarily entered mental health inpatient care. Her troubles included attachment disorders as well some for-real schizophrenic breaks from reality.

"Do you mean Jenny?" he shot at the men.

"Ah, well pastor it would be quite inappropriate to name the individual in question. After all, she is not claiming anything other than mutual dalliance."

Carter was shocked. This was idiocy and cruelty. To everyone involved.

"Pastor Jons," a new voice spoke from the end of the table. "As counsel for the church, I must inform you of their intent to enact the moral failure clause of your retirement compensation agreement."

"Pastor," the head elder spoke again. "We would prefer to say as little as necessary on this. We need not drag you through the mud here. Yes, if a member inquires, we will be bound to share the basics. But only that the morality clause was enacted and church funds will not be going to the retirement accounts of our former, disgraced pastor. You've lost the employment suit. Do we need to make this any more painful than it already is?"

Carter had no words.

Trooper Jons' phone buzzed again.

This time it was a selfie of Theo and Mia, clutching their midsections dramatically, clearly fainting from hunger.

The two men at the table smiled and said goodbye. They picked up their books, thankful for the time they'd spent together.

Carter grabbed his stuff, walked up to the counter, and paid for the bag of coffee beans.

Then he headed home.

SEVENTEEN

Townsend hit "send."

It was an easy enough task while driving north on 75. He'd just made the turn at Topeka and was on the last third of his travels. It was his last check-in en route and made use of a simple emoji to let *The Family* know all was well. In reality, all was not. Two dead bodies held the possibility of discovery. He wasn't about to send any kind of clear messaging about that. Far too risky. Even given their communication protocols.

Townsend had a burner phone. Supplied by his cohorts, it had been programmed to send via a dark web app. The Feds thought they were so smart. This many years after 911, everyone was wise to the scam known as the Patriot Act. Nothing more than the most sweeping anti-privacy legislation ever enacted. All under the guise of safety.

People are so very afraid, Perry reflected. Fear makes you do dumb things.

He looked at his phone.

Send complete.

The largest government surveillance operation in the world was aimed at her own citizens. In supposedly the freest nation on the planet. But even the combined efforts of NSA, CIA, FBI, HSA and surely other alphabet-laden groups yet to be named couldn't follow the simple text he'd just sent. They'd break it someday. Likely in the next eighteen months. But all that was necessary was to stay ahead of the curve. Townsend didn't know who was in charge of the tech. Probably not anyone he'd ever meet.

Outside Denver, CO

The phone screen on the other end simply buzzed four times. No popup. No notification. Not even an actual text message in the inbox.

Three men sat in the enormous living space. The great-room ceiling stretched to twenty-five feet, bisected by fir beams and leading gracefully to full length picture windows. An alpine meadow filled the glass, even as the last rays of sunlight faded behind the mountaintop opposite.

"He's a little behind," the oldest said.

"Weather?" from another.

"I don't like it," the third stated. "We've been set back already."

"We're trusting you, you know."

The second man waited.

"He'll be fine. He'll make the connection this evening. A day and a half should still be plenty of time."

"Go show your father."

The eleven-year-old did as directed by his mother, walking into the great-room and breaking up the conversation.

"Hey, dad."

The oldest man lit up and spoke before the boy's father could reply.

"Well, well. Trey, you are certainly growing up fast. Have you mother's looks… thankfully."

The boy felt obliged to laugh.

"You staying out of trouble? Well, I mean for the most part, right? Remind me so much of my own son. But he's who know's where now."

"Uh, sorry to hear that," the boy offered.

"Well, you know. They grow up. Sometimes get their own ideas. But I am trusting the verse: 'Train up a child in the way he should go, and in the end he will not turn from it.' Say, you're in the Wilderness Corps, right? Is that a badge project you got there?"

"Yeah. Just finished. Mom wanted Dad to take a look before I turn it in. Heritage badge. Pretty much a family tree. I like the outdoor skills stuff better, but it was kinda interesting."

"I know what you mean," the older man continued. "But where you come from is nothing to be taken lightly, son. If you don't mind," he looked to his father, "tell me what you found?"

The dad nodded.

"Sure. Well these parts of the diagram appear in northern England, about Twelfth Century. Miners. Pretty sure of that connection but it's harder to tell the farther back you go."

"Yes, that's very true," he pointed, "The fur cap icon?"

"Super cool. One of our ancestors was a frontiersman, an army scout right before the war of independence. He was one of three men who regularly reported on British supply lines. Most of the big raids used his info. Those ships are another part of our family that stayed in England. Owned a big shipping operation. Africa and back. Must've been some crazy adventures. Trace the timeline and that's a big tobacco farm in Kentucky, 1840s. Lots of names there.

Some are a little hard to pronounce. Even found some business documents. Yellowed, lots of edges torn. But, man. I think for that time, they were rich."

A quick look around the main floor confirmed that trendline had continued to current day.

They returned to the diagram. Two main lines jutted from there. One landing in Colorado. The other, California.

"Depression was hard on our family, like most folks," the boy picked up again. "That's how we got here," his smaller finger landed just outside of Denver. "Dad's dad's dad… " he stopped to check for accuracy "started up the mill. When things got running, great-grandma and their kids followed, a year later."

"That's great, thorough work" his dad finally stepped in. "Let me check it off," he grabbed a pen, "and then it's about time for dinner, right?"

The boy wasn't about to prolong what amounted to extracurricular homework when a homemade pizza was just coming out of the oven. He took the signed sheet and nearly ran to the dining table.

"He asking yet?" the older man muted his voice.

"California line? No, not really. All he knows at this point is we lost contact with that side of the family. Lots of folks had trouble staying connected after heading west, so we just had him gray it out. Let him know that the things we can track clearly are more important than things we can't. Seems to be okay with that for now."

"That's what I thought, too," the older man lectured. "And look what happened to my… "

"Sure," the father pressed. "We'll talk. But he's eleven. How is he supposed to think about his grand-uncle turning on everyone, everything our line had known, accomplished… for the better part of centuries. All because he got religion? We already had it! What did some tent-revival preacher give him that an education and family money couldn't? We were elders, leaders in our churches, for heaven's sake. Pillars of the community before those… those self-righteous hypocrites. Tell me why a factory with endless hours and not enough pay to even make rent is better than a family farm where everyone is taken care of."

The dad caught his voice rising and settled down.

The older man smiled. "Yes. I think we're going to be okay. Your replacement will do fine, I'm sure. I see it in your face, your heart. You wouldn't have it any other way. Thirty-six hours. Your family, our family. The line will only grow stronger."

North of Topeka

Townsend knew nothing of the stories. He only knew his. And he knew what he was doing was for the best. For everyone. Pain and trial are inherent in growth. He hadn't needed that lesson, he'd lived it. Resurrection leads to purpose. This, too, he had come to experience firsthand as the three men in the great-room had come to his aid in that lonely, cold hospital room only a few years ago. Five hours more of this insufferable gray pavement was a small price to pay, given the immeasurable gains he would win for those he now called kin.

EIGHTEEN

The room was electric.

"The *senator?* You've confirmed this with her people?"

"Just got off the phone with them. Security team will be here tonight. They want access to everything. Files, personnel. The arena. It's a quick speech, five minutes max, and then a wave and goodbye. Still, we've got a lot to go over if we want to make this happen."

"So, they're probably going over our social media, right?"

This one came from the back of the room but everyone was thinking it.

"Yeah," Dennis nodded.

No one told them that stuff would stay around forever. Or at least, they didn't think it would matter when they started posting anything and everything. Most had developed some form of broadcast filter over the years. Most. But nothing online is every truly scrubbed.

"Well," a striking blonde offered. "Most of you have nothing to worry about. It's not like everyone in this room hasn't done some campaign work the last few elections. They do most of that background before letting you anywhere near a candidate."

"Yep," Dennis affirmed. "Shouldn't be a problem. Unless, of course," he mocked "some of you voted for you-know-who last time around. That would be a big mistake. Yuuuuuuge." The senior member of the conference committee got some laughs on that one. Most knew him well from his PoliSci courses at Creighton. Tenured professor. Social justice blogger. Very part-time activist. That last part he tried to keep as quiet as possible. "Terri here will handle the interface with the senator's people," he glanced toward the blonde. "Everything goes through her. Ben?"

"Dr. Paulsen, yeah."

"You can just call me Dennis here, Ben."

"Sure."

"What are we moving to make room for the senator?"

"Uh, well looks like we had a video up top of the speaking order."

"The opening video or the feature on redlining?"

"Opening video. Conference branding. Thematic setup."

"Ah, we can't ditch that. We have to grab everyone from the first seconds. That's a great piece. Can we slide the senator in right after?"

"Yep. But then we've got the first keynote. Justice Studies guy from Brown. Was super hard to get him in the first place. How will he feel about getting bumped?"

"Seriously?" Terri jumped in. "Nebraska's first female senator is showing up to our conference and you're concerned about hurting a man's feelings? Please tell me we're past this kind of thing."

A tentative voice came forward. "So, she's the second woman senator from Nebraska… "

"Does. Not. Count." Terri shot back. "First one with a D by her name. Which means first one to represent women."

"Okay," Dennis stepped in. "So, Terri here will contact our other esteemed guest and let him know we've had a change to the program."

"Oh, trust me," she said. "Not a problem. Win-win. The senator and a chance to check the patriarchy? I will definitely enjoy this."

Not everyone in the room concurred.

"Hey, Dennis."

"Yeah?" he turned, halfway from their meeting room, down the hall.

"Ah, sorry. I know we're on a quick break, but can we talk a second?"

"Sure, Ben. In here?" a side room was open.

"Thanks. I'll make this quick. Are you sure about the senator. I mean, yeah, she's a really high profile snag for us… "

"But?"

"Maybe it's just a timing thing. I don't know, seems weird to ever pass up an opportunity like this. Still, she's a little… hot, right now."

"You mean the reparations bill? That where you're going with this?"

"Um, yeah. And after the midterms, this could be more than just pressing her bonafides with the base. The committees are lined up to get it at least a few steps forward."

"And you see this as a problem?"

"Look, you know me, Dr.…."

"Dennis."

"Dennis. I appreciate that you've allowed me to work alongside you. Research has been amazing. Even though I am a… "

"A Christian?"

"Yeah, exactly. We both know my faith informs my work. Undergirds it. Informs it at every step. There are some places we disagree. This would be one of them."

"So you think reparations are a *bad* idea."

"Not the idea. Not necessarily. But I've seen the outline of her bill."

"Sure, so have I."

"Okay, *so* much of it makes no practical sense, whatsoever. The blood tests. Yikes, I mean I guess you have to confirm eligibility somehow but the optics on that one are not completely un-Nuremberg. Nebraska wasn't a slave state, so we'd be redirecting citizens' money in some weird disproportion. And how do we even quantify whether someone four generations back would have been successful with equivalent resources? Seems like we're just assuming the case? I am all for acknowledgment of the past and the trajectories set in motion by it. But this? This is the kind of thing that divides, not unites. Isn't that what we're doing here? The marquee outside says 'reconciliation' not 'revolution.'"

"Ben," the professor put his hand on his shoulder. "As always, I appreciate your thoughtfulness. And I understand your concerns. Really, I do. But there are times in any movement when momentum is pushed into action. I think this is one of those times. You've told me more than once, quite boldly, that you believe God wants justice to prevail. You've quoted Jesus' words to me about 'on earth as it is in heaven.' Maybe, just maybe—and you know I am not a believer—your god is doing something big in the next couple of days. Hmmm?"

Ben was silent.

"Now, we've got to get back on those pesky conference details, don't we?"

The deed had been done.

"So, how did *Professor Brown* take it?"

"He pouted," Terri reported. "At least at first. He's got a book coming out. Was hoping this would be a big splash."

"Sheesh. So much for pure motivations," another committee member added.

"But he's still coming, obviously," she said.

"Of course he is," Dennis replied. "Not many chances to speak to ten thousand eager conferees." Dr. Paulsen left it unsaid that he would also be speaking, closing the gathering Saturday afternoon. He didn't have a book coming out next month. It was outlined, yes. But not yet written, at least.

"Anyone else… " Ben offered tiredly.

"Done for today?" Dennis completed the thought. "Yep. I'd say that's a great afternoon of work. Getting really, really close to go-time, even with the new and exciting happenings. Let's finish up any last items in the next fifteen, shall we? You're all doing amazing work here. So thankful for each of you."

Twenty minutes later the building was dark.

Terri sat alone as her car warmed up in the community center parking lot where they'd met over the last three months. She was tired but feeling her skill, her presence, was needed more than ever now. She watched the line of ice melt from the bottom up on her windshield and let the growing warmth close her eyelids for just a second.

"Hey, Terri."

Startled, she turned to her left.

"Oh hey, sorry," Ben offered. "Just saw you sitting here for a few minutes and wondered if everything was okay."

"Oh, Ben," she breathed. "Yeah, you surprised me alright. All good. Just trying to get warm before I take off. Hate driving with cold air blowing around."

"Totally know what you're talking about. Okay, then. See you tomorrow."

"Absolutely," she smiled. "See you tomorrow."

Two minutes later a phone buzzed.

No message. No image. Just four short buzzes.

The father with the big home in the mountains noted it calmly, setting it aside for the rest of his family dinner.

NINETEEN

"CJ?"

Mae waited a beat.

"Carter?"

Nothing.

"Carter. Jons. Carter Rupert Jons the Third, *Esquire*?"

"That's not daddy's name," Theo laughed. Mia was almost too cool for it all.

"Ah," Carter leaned on his right elbow, spoon to lips. Then he set the utensil down, grabbed his water glass, and sipped.

Still nothing.

"You've got to be kidding me," Mae said.

"What?" he finally focused on the small dining table and his family around it.

"Soooooo. How was the new coffee shop? The beans smelled great. I'd whip up some after dinner but they're not decaf."

"Oh, yeah. Ah, great little place. Did some reading. Saw some guys doing a Bible study there," he stared again.

"Excellent report, Trooper Jons. Other evidence to enter into the record?"

"Not at this time, your honor," he played along.

"But you do have some items you would like to enter into the dishwasher, correct?"

"Indeed I do," he was picking up the pace as he stood, scooting back his chair. "And I will need some assistance from my junior troopers, as well."

General ughhhs followed by shuffling of feet.

"Awesome," Mae added. "I believe my sentence for cooking a fantastic meal is thirty minutes on the couch with the newest issue of Magnolia Magazine."

"And people says there's no justice in this world," Carter finished.

Half an hour was enough for the dishes but not nearly enough to clear Carter's head. He walked into the living room. Mae knew the look.

"Hey, sorry. Just so much going on. Mind if I take a run before the kids go to bed?"

"I don't know, Carter. I liked my slightly doughy pastor better than this newly toned policeman. Let's keep things reasonable, okay?"

He knew she was joking. He had talked about losing fifteen forever. But in his old job there were so many meetings. So little movement. So many treats brought by during the week, not to mention what was offered at home visits. It would be rude to decline, right? As a trooper, most shifts had him out and about. Sure, much of the time was still sitting in his cruiser, but there were plenty of walkarounds and many days included some form of workout, however brief, at the district station. The well-worn picture of donuts and bulging utility belts was as fictional as every-other-moment foot chases and jaw-dropping leaps over chain link fencing. He was new. Still, he hoped for at least one of those. And a donut would be allowed, now and then.

Carter smiled as he headed down to the basement. The partially finished space had concrete brick walls with a bathroom and laundry area behind studs and drywall. He'd always felt silly stretching, even in school sports. It seemed goofy. Now he knew it was vital. His older body needed to know what was coming. After a few minutes, the treadmill called his name. Black earbuds seated into both canals. He plugged in the red safety key, set the pace for a good jog, and stepped onto the tread.

It felt good to run. His breathing increased. Blood pumped throughout his body, more oxygenated with every stride. He remembered back to his first few workouts, prior to the academy. While pastoring he had allowed himself to drift into the poorest shape of his life. He knew the twenty weeks of training would tax him, that he was going to have to work harder than all the younger candidates. But if he was going to be the old guy, he was going to be the old guy they all had to keep up with. So, he bought the treadmill off of Facebook Marketplace and got to it.

It had taken a while but he'd actually experienced the runner's high once or twice. Even if that wasn't commonplace, he always felt better after a run. Clearer. More settled.

Tonight that was not the case.

Please be informed that civil court proceedings…

He replayed the board scene where they accused him of infidelity. Couldn't get it out of his head. Even though he'd just been exonerated. Well, not exonerated because he'd never been "charged" of anything. That's the problem with civil cases. It was enough to file a complaint. If there was reasonable context, it had to play out, at least a little bit. He should be thankful. Relieved.

He wasn't.

He was angry.

His hand reached over to the speed setting, punching it up a bit. His feet dug in, each step pulling at the rubber mat, throwing it forcefully behind only to come back around again.

He saw their smug faces. Their self-righteous postures.

More speed.

He started breathing heavier, sweating down his back.

Can't this thing go any faster?

Max speed.

His heart burned the same way as the moment he'd faced their accusations. Not all of the men on the board were so aggressive about his departure and his reputation. A few he'd considered friends. A couple of them had marriages falling apart and he'd spent extra efforts in counseling and care. Their kids weren't perfect, just like everyone else. There were nights at the hospital. Aging parents. What parts of their lives had he not entered into deeply, regularly?

Carter hit the volume button on the console and music filled his ears. Drums and guitars matched his heartbeats, even as worship lyrics tried to shout down his thoughts. When he'd first tried to introduce some new instruments at church, he thought *that* would be his biggest battle. He would have bartered now for a hundred of those, compared to what eventually unfolded.

In his mind, he was running away from it all. But he wasn't going anywhere. Same steps, no matter how hard he pushed. Aching. Burning. Still, he had more. He wasn't through with them yet. He couldn't believe they'd go so far. The news had dropped that very evening, spreading throughout the congregation. The phone started ringing. After five brutal conversations, he gave up answering. Mae never wavered. She knew her husband. She knew he was mortal, yes. She also knew this was just plain ridiculous.

The next weeks the kids got pulled into it as well. Mia was confused. Theo just knew he couldn't play with his best friends anymore.

How dare you! In what world do you imagine this kind of act as good or holy? Jesus called the Pharisees whitewashed tombs. I wouldn't even waste the space on you.

His feet slapped hard, fists pumping, chest heaving.

Stop.

He punched the speed control, grabbed the handholds, and pulled his feet to the side. He yanked the earbuds out, letting them fall. The machine slowed, gliding to a stop. Carter wanted to scream. He knew that would upset the kids. So, he grabbed a towel and walked into the laundry room, muffling shouts while sopping up perspiration.

He so wanted to feel better. He didn't.

TWENTY

He'd slept a few hours.

Justyn awoke hungry. His stomach didn't so much growl as simply ache.

He'd started to feel it earlier. The list of bodily concerns was growing. While the young man was doing his best to set aside the present trials and focus on the mission, he found himself dulling. For a while he was able to reset his mind by reciting the principles *The Family* had instilled in him.

Yes, it takes a village: your village.

They weren't averse to helping one another. On the contrary. Others often remarked at their extraordinary generosity and presence in each others' lives. More than once members of their group had been commended publicly for acts of bravery, loyalty. They would even save the lives of those not in their orbit if needed. Outsiders were human and deserved life as well. But they deserved a separate life, one where they could achieve the basics: family, work. It was not the goal of *The Family* to vanquish. Their destiny, instead, was to rule.

Justyn needed some help understanding the mission in this context. Placement in the arena's structural workings ensured massive casualties. How was this not a contradiction?

In reply, he'd been offered a Bible story.

Nehemiah had been gone a number of years.

The ancient Jewish leader had accomplished his primary goals of resettling the city of Jerusalem after their banishment to Babylon, and later Persia. As cupbearer to the king, he returned to his duties, leaving leaders in place to continue their progress. He left successfully. Now, he was back. And he was not pleased.

The list of failures was long. Their temple had been defiled, space rented to the key antagonist of Nehemiah's earlier work. The people had neglected the Law. They were no longer loyal to Yahweh. But, most egregious: they had intermarried with surrounding peoples. Pagans. Followers of the Baals.

Non-Jews.

"Justyn," his teacher had probed. "Do you see what came of this single, seemingly innocent act? Surely the Jews loved their spouses. One cannot fault them for being attracted. But that is why they were warned, sternly, against it."

"I am not sure I understand yet. I want to."

"Let me ask another question. Could they all have lived in peace?"

"It seems so."

"How? Imagine another scenario."

"I think they could have managed if they'd just stayed in their own clans around Jerusalem."

"Yes, Justyn. And what kind of city is Jerusalem?"

"Ah… well, Jewish."

"Correct. Jewish city. Jewish customs. Jewish god. Jewish… "

"Control?"

Justyn thought another second. "So, why are so many Jewish people today doing the exact opposite? They don't seem to be fighting for their own. They seem to be fighting the very things we know are right. Embracing multiculturalism, diversity, even in their politics."

"Well, some have, yes. They've forgotten. Forgotten who they are."

Justyn struggled with the story. Surely his elder was not advocating for another group than theirs to hold superiority. He guessed, instead, that all metaphors fall apart at some point.

Justyn continued thinking out loud. "The conference. They are not just people willing to live in peace. They're the ones not willing to leave well enough alone."

"See? A little reflection often leads to understanding on our own terms. Something much deeper than just being told. Excellent. Yes. I do wish they'd left well enough alone. But they have not. And so we have no choice. Their influence may not yet have gained momentum. Soon, though. Better for some than an entire nation to perish."

Justyn coughed.

This time his whole upper body moved violently.

As did the van.

The previous falls had been slow. This most certainly was not. 9,000 pounds of steel and glass had been teetering on the edge for the past two hours, much of the time Justyn had been sleeping. Meanwhile, the underground creek ate away at the densely packed snow and ice. Little by little its crystalline building blocks weakened. The tipping point had been reached and it slid quickly, an ugly, poorly balanced bobsled in full motion.

The small space he'd inhabited groaned with the forces around him. The van was bottoming out, cast by gravity onto and between the several large rocks at water's edge. Like the inside of a can under pressure he watched the walls and ceiling approach, baring torn edges, threatening to slice him into pieces. He pulled as much air in as he could. It hurt so bad. He coughed more. He screamed.

And then it stopped.

Justyn's chest heaved.

"No!" he cried out. "No! This can not be happening!"

The young man had made peace with the upturned vehicle a day ago. Had even come to feel like he was mastering his space, achieved some sense of control. Now he was stuck. His head was pinned to the left. His left arm was caught at his side, maybe a few inches of room. His right arm was more free but set at an odd angle, away from his waistline. The cabin had compressed into a for-real casket, with Justyn immobilized in an upward, slightly supine position. As he began to assess the situation he breathed thanks for one thing and one thing only. He was not upside down himself.

Breathing.

His thanks just doubled. The tree limb bringing him air over the last day and a half was somehow still intact. It had, in fact, shifted even closer to his head with the fall.

But beyond those simple mercies, Justyn's plan for survival had just melted away. He'd wondered how much time he had before using the second heat pouch. That choice had been made for him. Using his right arm he found the packet, nearly halfway out of his parka pocket. Could have been so much worse. There was no way his left arm was going to swing over enough to use both hands. The warmer needed to be torn open.

Guess this is why we have teeth.

The strain was almost unbearable. Three times he'd gotten the edge within an inch of his right incisor. But then he saw stars and his hand fell away, ragdoll-esque.

"Ah…" he reached again. "So… so … close."

He bit down as hard as he could and pulled away with his gloved hand. He missed and was met for his efforts with a spray of blood from a gash on his desert-like lips. His mouth filled with red. Iron. The metallic taste made him gag. He coughed and spit. His head spun more.

One last pull with literally everything he had.

Tooth pierced packaging. He moved his head the little he could. A chunk of plastic fell from his mouth. A small glow, then growing. Justyn blinked. Then tears.

Remarkably, his encasing had not resulted in further injury. And the closeness of the van's crumpled remains would keep the heat more efficiently. But it was a small victory in the face of certain death. The timeline had started. He knew it now. There would be no rescue. No escape. His mind would need to shift entirely to his untimely end. Would there be valor? Would he be victorious for himself and *The Family*, regardless of his demise?

There was nothing else. The odd, singular focus constrained. Not in a bad way. Less to consider. From here on out only the necessary would occupy him. His years would end, his story close, in a small patch of trees in the middle of nowhere. It would take a certified miracle to end otherwise. And, while *The Family*'s god was quite capable of such, they more often looked to his help only and after they helped themselves.

TWENTY ONE

"Hey, that was quick."

Carter looked back at his wife, already leaning back in bed with a book in her lap.

"You know, you can talk to me, babe," she offered.

"Yeah. Wasn't the best run I've ever had," he stepped into the small ensuite bathroom.

"Ah. I was talking about the kids. That must have been one of the speediest last trains to sleepy town ever. Got them both tucked in?"

"Oh. The kids."

"Yes. Kids. Our children."

"Mae," he smiled. "Yes, Our children. In bed. All good."

"C'mon, Carter. What's going on? You're even edgier than usual."

He needed to talk. Still, some male weirdness from generations ago kept him from opening his mouth to the very one he needed to lean into most. *I can do this on my own* was the mantra every man fought, mostly on the inside. *I should be able to do this on my own* was even more prevalent and twice as damaging. If the run downstairs illustrated anything, it was that he was very near the breaking point.

Carter was still too warm from the run and he wasn't about to take a cold shower in the middle of winter, so he just sat on top of the comforter.

"Okay," he started. "Topic one."

"Do I need pen and paper? There's a list? Will there be a test?"

That last one was unnecessary. She would track every last detail, but not just the facts. She'd follow his emotions, or at least as much as he'd allow himself.

"Topic one," he restated. "Work. There's some weird stuff going on. I know I'm still on the short side of experience but a few things feel, well just off to me."

"That's not a bad thing, CJ. Intuition. Hunches. Those have got to count for something, right?"

"Well, kind of. Mostly we're required to work in the world of evidence. Facts."

"And you don't have any of those right now?"

"Again, kind of."

"Babe, you're gonna need to fill me in a little more than that if you want a good listening partner."

He thought for a second. Nothing about the van "case" was privileged. Mostly, because there was no case to begin with.

"So, yesterday. I came back from over by McClelland."

"Hang on, CJ. What were you doing over there? I thought you were out on the interstate. In that weather? Two-lane road?"

"Ummm, yes. We get assigned to side roads now and then. Rookie gets the garbage runs."

He continued. "So, After McClelland, and yes, bad weather, we were reviewing camera feeds back at District. An old cargo van came up, first at the Love's stop a bit north and then the Underwood rest stop. Not so weird, so far."

"Understatement."

"I thought you wanted to listen."

"I do. But I'm pretty sure I just heard a rooster crow. Let's keep it moving?"

"Haha."

She smiled.

"So, van has one set of plates at Love's. Different set at Underwood. Next thing we check is footage prior to the first image. Okay, Buckner Feed and Seed... "

"Buckner Feed and Seed?"

"Sign on the side. Nice logo. But we have nothing. I mean, nothing prior to Love's. And the company has no trace, either. No web presence at all."

"That is a little weird. Go on, trooper Jons."

"Thank you. I thought so as well. I went back over the footage last night after putting the kids down. You were already asleep with the news on so I thought I'd give it another few minutes. Nothing, again. Then, today I'm on patrol and it hits me. What if that van wasn't actually on the road before Love's? What if it was being towed or on a car rack?"

"So, you went back and checked... "

"Well. Yeah, but not actually me. Shift sergeant put Bradford on it."

"Ah, and so now we are at Topic Two?"

Carter shrugged.

"Honey," Mae started. "Bradford? That must have gone over well. The way you've painted things, I am surprised you came home with both arms attached."

"Well, that's super violent. And, please, I could take her."

Mae cocked her head disbelievingly.

"Alright, alright. Yeah, she's a regional MMA champ in her spare time. But that's completely irrelevant."

"Only if I don't want a husband with two arms."

"So… like I was saying. Bradford ran the search again. No vans in tow that match. The kicker is that we just had another HomeSec flag this morning, as well."

"Feds? I thought you took that all with a grain of salt."

"Honestly, yeah I do. But this feels a little different. Like something's going on. Something bad."

"Have you prayed about it? Maybe the Spirit is prompting you, babe."

"Look, yes I am praying. Well, some of the time. But the last thing I need is to be painted as some religious nutbag, doing police work by visions and "leading.""

"Well, yeah, I wouldn't put it that way either. Still… "

Carter was equally thankful and irritated.

This was his work. His area. He didn't like the insinuations. He also noted he was feeling a little better as he talked.

"Topics One and Two." Mae said after a pause. "Gotta be more there, right babe?"

He knew he should share the email from his lawyer. She would be relieved, right? So why was he still holding it back?

"Alright, yes. Topic Three for whoever is counting."

Mae motioned "topic three" with an imaginary pad and pen.

"The Roth account. Lawyer emailed me."

Mae sat up.

"Case dismissed. No evidence to support the," he had a hard time even saying it. "Moral failure clause."

He glanced her way.

"That's not news at all," she proclaimed. "Stupidest legal action in the history of legal actions. Can't believe it took this long. Carter," she looked straight into his eyes. "You, Mr. Carter Jons are my husband, whom I love and trust. The Lord brought us together. It's been a bit of a weird ride, yes, but I am so glad He seated us together. I have never, *ever* doubted your innocence and I am so incredibly sorry for what they did to you…"

He sensed there was more. "But?… "

"Not a 'but'. An 'and,'" she added. "And I think it's time to leave it all behind, don't you? I mean, isn't that the core of all your stress? I have never read the Psalms more personally than these last few years. Betrayal. Deception. Usurping. Disrespect. All in the name of some weak-sauce fundamentalist legalism that apparently knows no bounds. And Christ's words about leaven? Spot on. We literally watched a sweet, small family of Jesus followers get taken over by a few disgruntled locals with a record of going from church to church and killing them from the inside out. Someone needs to help them see that they might be the problem. I mean, if I… "

"Whoa, Mae." Carter laughed. That one felt good. He stopped and grabbed her hands. "I have no idea what I would have done without you. Without the kids. And yeah, without the Lord. I couldn't agree more. It's time to leave that season behind. I know I need to pray more about… well, the church thing."

"Excellent," she leaned in for a kiss. "So, that could be Topic Four. Tomorrow should be a fine opportunity to take a step in the right direction."

Oh yeah, tomorrow. School day off. The church play day.

TWENTY TWO

Approaching Omaha

Townsend's heart sped upon seeing the road sign.

D *owntown, all exits.*
His butt thanked him, as well.

It had been one very long day. Idledale, Colorado was so very far behind now. Passing by Denver, endless road to Topeka. North and now, his mission was fully in sight.

The curve of the highway took him right past CHI Health Arena. Few lights were on at this hour. Night security and cleaning were sparsely in view. Perry saw a chubby rent-a-cop heading up the middle concourse. Nothing unusual, at least from here. That was good news. Very good news.

The day had been long. It had not been uneventful. Perry's actions were still unknown. All he needed was another forty-eight hours of luck. Or providence. Maybe a mix of both. The fact he had come this far without discovery made him think it was more of the latter.

He pulled past the stadium and headed north of town. Once off the interstate, he followed a maze of one-way streets. The urban core faded behind as he drove among steel pole buildings, empty lots, very few residences—those few looked largely uninhabited.

Perry pulled up to the back fence of the lot.

As promised, the smaller chainlink gate opened.

Richards let him through and then swung it closed. He jogged ahead as Townsend took the curve slow at the last row of units. Three digits opened the large metal door again and van #2 arrived, late but not too late.

Perry shut the engine off and stepped out and down onto painted concrete.

The immediate quiet unsettled him.

"Man, that was a lot of road."

Richards put his hand up.

"Ah, okay. I'm Per… "

Richards put another hand up.

"Look," Richards started. "I don't care. I'm here to do a job. That may offend you, being all pure and such but we are not going to become friends. Matter of fact," he pulled his jacket back, handgun at his waist, "I'd prefer to know as little as possible about you. And if I get the sense you know too much about me, we will have a bad parting. Solid?"

Townsend was taken aback. He'd been briefed that his partner onsite would not be a member of *The Family*. But they did have to work together, at least minimally.

"Cool, yeah. I just thought… "

"No. No thinking, just doing."

Richards walked around back of the van. He pulled up short. "You've got to be kidding me."

How in the world did I miss that? Townsend glared.

"When did that happen?" Richards insisted. "You know how quick you'll get pulled over for a busted tail light? You made it this far? Do you even know when it happened? How am I supposed to work with someone so stupid?"

Townsend knew not to speak.

Richards seethed for another second. Then he remembered the paycheck. "Aghhhh. Not a great start. Not great at all. You are so lucky I have another one here. You want an evidence trail? How about heading over to the local auto parts store and buying a replacement lamp for a Ford Transit?"

"I... I don't know when that happened. Maybe a rock or something? Lots of road today. Lots of cars. Snow and ice flying all over the place."

Richards stepped closer, staring. "If there's something I need to know. Something that would make it harder for me to do my job. I need to know. *Now*."

Another pause.

"I will wait."

Townsend's assurances worked for now.

The big rolling door on the back of the van came up. There were surprisingly few items for what they were about to set into motion. Ten five-gallon containers. They barely took up the first third of the space. Nearly half of the remainder held cardboard boxes. Each one a cubic foot. Nothing menacing. No indications externally of their collective power. Richard's specialization was not a matter of brute force. The ability to get as much material in place for the desired effect was not just impractical, it was impossible. The math wasn't addition. Not even multiplication. It was exponential.

He was by education an electrical engineer. The chemistry was important but not critical. Instead, a compounding array of small charges would give him the overwhelming and desired outcome. If Troy had smuggled a small army in via their horse, he currently laid his eyes on the modern equivalent of a battlefield atomic weapon in the back of a cargo van. The clear advantages here were no fallout after the fact and no danger of radiation while handling. His device was also significantly less expensive to build and much easier to hide. In short, it was a marvel.

Satisfied, he closed the door and got to work.

Rubbing alcohol at the edges. Cleanup work with a small utility knife. Careful color blending from road wear. It came off in one piece. Good. He walked over to the workbench and pulled a large carton from underneath. The utility knife sliced the box lid clean. Richards took the items over to the side of Townsend's van and held them up, confirming size and placement. Two minutes with a hair dryer on the van's side. Then he walked back over to the workbench, pulling two toothpaste-like tubes from a bag. Opening them, he mixed an even amount of the blue and gray on a small patch of cardboard. With sure strokes, the color and texture became more uniform. A strong odor lifted from his work. He didn't care or simply ignored it. Perry covered his nose.

Satisfied with the batch, Richards grabbed the cardboard and walked back over beside the van. Using a small brush he layered some of the substance where he'd placed blue painter's tape as reference. Then he added some to the back of the items he'd pulled from under the bench. He lifted one and set it against the van's side. A level showed the need for a slight adjustment on the horizontal. Richards was, after all, a perfectionist.

He looked at his phone for thirty seconds and then let go.

Walking to the other side, he repeated the last few steps.

Buckner Feed and Seed became *MidTown Digital*.

The two vans had their ticket in. They also had their full complement of explosives.

THURSDAY

TWENTY THREE

The dog pulled more than usual this morning.

It was difficult to walk, let alone run.

"Stop it. Just, aghhhh, stop."

The owner adjusted his handhold on the leash. He'd even bought one of those spikey collars, supposed to give the dog a little bit of physical feedback. Not pain, just knowing when he was to cease and re-center on his master's body and voice. Honestly, he'd paid for training, done everything he was supposed to. Most days the border collie mix did fine. She was getting better, especially with more frequent practice. But she was still technically a pup, so there was that.

The dog insisted. She moved relentlessly in the opposite direction of their walk and almost free of the collar. He was trying to reign her in even more. Flicked the thumbhold on the leash control. It opened instead of closed. She bolted, the line playing out as fast as it could, and then a sudden jerk at its end.

"Great. Now, look what you've done."

The man stepped into the edge of the bramble. He wouldn't be able to untangle it all without unclipping her.

"You've really got this all messed up. Wait. Look at me. Stay. Staaay."

She ran again, this time down into the steep edge of the ravine. With no effort she raced over, under, through downed limbs and all that makes its way to the forest floor.

Then, she stopped.

The Jefferson County Sheriff's Office arrived within minutes.

"Hey, leave it."

"What?"

"The snow. Leave it in place. Brushing it off like that could move evidence."

"Seriously?"

"Yeah. Look, I know this is not a routine occurrence out here so you'll just need to trust me on this. Twenty in Philly taught me a few things, even if it did ruin pretty much the rest of my life."

"So, what? We just wait until spring?"

"Jackson," the detective sergeant called up the hill. "Get me a hairdryer."

"Come again?"

"A hairdryer. Run a power cord from your unit. Get on it, now."

Twenty minutes later a line of three extension cords snaked from the squad car's 110 outlet in the trunk, down the hill, and to a salon-worthy piece of equipment courtesy of a very concerned but very nice woman in the closest home on the street.

Snow melt ran off the left foot of the deceased. It was a wonder they'd even found him. Yes, the shoe size was far too large for a female, at least on average. The DS scanned the immediate area. Snow, leaves, branches. If not for the dog's keen sense of smell, they would have been waiting until the first good thaw.

"Well, that works way better than I thought."

The detective sergeant let the comment go. This was not his first body. For the younger deputy, clearly, it was. He was a little too excited. That wouldn't last long. Lifeless human bodies were the ugliest thing on the planet. Deceased was a good clinical term, and it got at the idea of an abrupt stop. But the degree of what had ended was always the harder punch. Language, thinking, work, play, relationships. It all suddenly, and irreversibly, ceased. Legs, waistline, torso appeared as he continued his work. Above the neck would be the worst.

"Oh, my," the younger officer stepped back, grabbing at his mouth and covering it.

"You know him."

"Sarge. That's Brewer. Hank Brewer. Machine shop guy across the street. What in the… "

The DS kept at it, working the last area still covered. He carefully set aside a clump of branches and pine. The color contrast was shocking, pure white against deep red.

"Son, I need you to be certain here. Brewer?"

The man's face lay upward, a vacant stare. It was the clearest and most profound indication of a world not what it was created to be. The end-run of hubris.

"Okay," the DS shot back up the hill. "We have a Mr. Hank… "

"Uh… Henry, sir. Henry."

"Thank you, deputy. Mr. *Henry* Brewer, deceased. The clock is ticking. We need to find out who and why, and whether there is still a danger present in our community. Scene?" he asked specifically.

"They're here, sir," from up top. "Heading down the trail now. It's a little easier that way with their gear."

The older man slipped off latex gloves and set down the dryer.

"Sir?"

"Yeah."

"Not an accident? For sure?"

"Son, I am not trying to belabor a horrifying situation. But… take another look. Seem like an accident to you?"

The Crime Scene Unit got to work.

It was gruesome, detailed labor. There were no immediate discoveries. Just lots of small bags filled with even smaller pieces of evidence. And much of it wouldn't lead to anything. But in the aggregate, it would paint a picture. That picture would be used to think about the frame. And the frame might very well lead to solving the crime.

The DS stood by, catching a final few questions with the man whose dog made the untimely discovery. Police cars nearest the edge of the ravine had all but finished up their duties. A lonely flare still glowed on the icy, wet road, keeping passersby to a single lane, and out of direct line of sight. Yellow tape stretched for twenty or so feet, marking the path down the hill and through the brush.

Just then a rope pulled a rescue basket up and into the clear. It was a cruel irony but the best way they had to extract Mr. Brewer's corpse. The frigid temps had done what a morgue cooler would. Initial examination revealed the advantage of a small window of time since death. As brutal as it sounded, the fresher the better, as far as these things went. The medical examiner had been notified and he wanted the corpse brought from icy setting to lab as quickly as possible.

The dog owner watched the bagged body loaded in and off in a matter of seconds.

"I am so sorry you had to see all of this," the DS redirected.

"Me, too. Me, too. I …" he struggled with a thought. "I heard he lived right around here."

"Actually, he worked here. Lived about ten minutes away. I really hate to do this, but just a couple more questions and we'll be good."

The man nodded. His dog sat obediently, taking cues from his master's body language.

"This is not your normal run?"

"Uh, yeah. I mean, correct. No, I usually run through the woods over by Cedar Lodge. It's closed for trail maintenance. I saw this walk on a list on the town visitor's website. Horrible luck. Or maybe it's good I was here? I don't know… "

"It's definitely good you were here. That's all I need for now. We've got all your contact info. Please be ready to answer a call or visit if we need more. Again, I am so very sorry you had to see this. But thank you for all your help."

"You're going to… uh, going to get whoever did this, right?"

"You've given us a great start."

The man walked away and the older officer paused for just a second, knowing they had a very good chance but no guarantees.

TWENTY FOUR

Justyn shivered. The warmth faded, like a fire's last embers.

Nearly an hour ago he woke up. Mid-morning held the slightest change in light, filtering down to where he lay some seventeen feet underground. While only his second full day of entrapment, the physical and emotional toil fit a more prolonged captivity.

The Family had prepared him for certain eventualities. Nothing he'd experienced after turning onto the farm road matched that list. There was questioning, both casual and prosecutorial. He knew what, and more importantly, what not to say. As a part-time driver for Buckner Feed & Seed, he knew very little. The details of this delivery only, along with the claims on the fake manifest. A few unrelated tidbits about the company but nothing that could be easily investigated. Nothing to arouse suspicions. There had even been a few sessions in which his life was mock-threatened. His first directive was to evade capture. Simply run. If a physical engagement could not be avoided he was ordered to fight. But he was not given a weapon. The states through which he was to travel had very different approaches to honoring the Second Amendment. He was prepared for a range of negative outcomes.

He was not ready for this.

He was not ready to die, alone and without honor.

Justyn wished he could reach his notebook. Now would be a fantastic time to sketch, to think, to reflect and strengthen himself in the ideals of his people. He couldn't see anything past his shoulder. The last waves of heat vanished from the pouch. Its nine hours had stretched into almost twelve. If that was a miracle, it wasn't enough.

He wasn't hungry anymore. He was very thirsty.

Justyn had fasted once in his life. On orders of the elders. In preparation for his rising ceremony, he had been told to take no food or drink for twenty-four hours. It was one of the hardest things he'd done in his short life. Twelve hours in he so wanted a cheeseburger. His head began to ache as the lack of water took its toll. Eighteen hours he felt weaker, still. Twenty hours he almost broke. It was crazy, reflecting on it later, how he couldn't even go a day like this when people across the globe regularly rose without food, only to go to bed the same. Water access and purity world over was one of the greatest sources of hospitalizations. He was soft. He was privileged. Neither were a curse, they just were. Unless he could find no way to overcome them to take up the mantle he had been given. So, he gritted his teeth for the final four hours. And then he went and got that cheeseburger. It didn't land well.

If he couldn't sketch, he could still imagine.

In his mind's eye he opened to a blank page. He pulled a pencil from its pouch. Setting the edge, he drew a fade across the top third. More rapid strokes brought texture. Then his hand guided the implement downward. Then across the middle. Trees. A brook. He created a sense of depth toward gently rolling hills. Back to the top where an orb glowed from above. He started the lettering. It worked beautifully into the scene, weaving in and out of the grassy meadow creekside.

Horizon comes for those who've battled the night.

Justyn was initially confused about the wording. Wouldn't that make more sense if you were fighting *through* the night?

An elder clarified the double meaning for him. Ah, yes. Night. Dark forces. Yes, that was more poetic.

"I've battled the night," he whispered.

The imagined page was ripped from him, violently.

In its place: sounds, horrors.

There was shrieking. Unholy cries of anguish. Phantoms flew past, left to right and back again. Some came from out front only to pass through him. His constrainment kept him from even wincing. He could not turn. He could not move. He certainly could not run. The visions compounded, like video streams out of sync, all vying for supremacy.

Justyn's heart raced and his head swam. If he had been standing surely he would have toppled. He heard chains and swore his feet had been manacled. All was a tempest and he leaned in, straining to make out any words, any semblance of reality.

He fought back.

"I've battled the night!" he cried out.

A gavel struck its sound block. The tone was distorted, wavering, and evolved into a scream. The most unearthly scream he had ever heard.

Justyn's ears caught the cracking.

His senses, though dulling, were mostly back online.

At first, the sound made a single punch. Then a spreading. Finally, an unimpressive descent and landing.

Justyn felt a rush of cold near his feet and a rush of air near his head. He heard a tinkle of water invading, forming a small pool. He couldn't see it but he knew what it meant. Despite numerous physical failings, the van's windshield had remained intact. This last defense had been conquered by weight and stress. The water would freeze. From the sound of the breach, more would cover its newly-solid surface. Maybe a quarter of an inch until it would also freeze, becoming the new and rising top. The process would repeat, at first below his feet. Then at his soles. Then his ankles. Up his legs in excruciating pain as flesh, nerves, and blood vessels gave way to exterior temperature. Slowly and agonizingly, he would become frozen in very small stages.

The burst of air by his head felt different than the supply he'd mercifully been granted to this point. Pocket, he thought. The limb has slipped as well, for the first time dipping beneath the surface of the snow above and falling into another cratered space. This precious resource, though potentially large, would be limited. How long? He had no way to tell.

He would either freeze to death or asphyxiate.

"I've battled the night," he whimpered. "At least I wasn't found. The mission will not fail."

Justyn had no more fight in him. He'd always been so sure of what waited on the other side. Still, it was different now that he was so very close. And what was that? A vision of hell? No, his mind was fading. Deprivations were taking their toll. He couldn't count on anything coming from his chemically-compromised gray matter. Maybe that would help, as the water breach would be a special torment of its own. One last test. At least it would be temporary. His reward would be eternal. Besides, if that was some kind of warning, he had no opportunity now for atonement, anyways. He'd forfeited that possibility long ago.

TWENTY FIVE

The Jefferson County Municipal Center was an all-in-one, brick exterior local government building.

The Medical Examiner had everything he needed. Just at a smaller scale. Ten individual cold lockers, the drawer system seen on every television show. A refrigerated room for autopsy and in rare occasions, overflow. With only seven current decedents in process, all were assured their own accommodations.

Toxicology came back fast, urged to the front of the line by the Sheriff's Department. Decomposition had been stalled, thanks to the cold. Nothing prevented a thorough physical and chemical roundup. There were no signs of death other than the glaringly obvious one at the back of the deceased's head. From the angle of impression the ME judged it as only one blow. One, very forceful and direct cranial impact. The resulting damage, both structurally and internally, was devastating.

Cause of death - blunt force, occipital trauma resulting in systemic bleed and pan-organ failure.

But then he finished his report with an odd note, one many doctors of his trade would miss.

Subdermal impression identified as consistent with tool end of machine ratchet.

"ME report in."

The detective sergeant pulled it up on screen. No surprises. While he wouldn't have ventured a guess at the actual tool, he knew where it had landed and that it had done the deed.

"Wait," he motioned. "Henry. Machine shop guy, right?"

"Yeah," a younger deputy confirmed.

"Machine ratchet sound like something he'd need in his shop?"

"Absolutely, sir. Heavy ones, too. Not like the ones you buy at the big box home stores. Direct from Kubota, others. Commercial sales."

"So, could be that Henry got it with his own piece of equipment."

He thought another second and continued.

"Time of death again was… "

"Between 3 and 5am," the deputy filled in.

"Ok. Henry's an early riser, like most sole proprietors. He's at the shop pre-dawn. In some yet unknown series of events, one of his very large, commercial grade ratchets is used against him."

"His shop was clean, boss. Nothing to indicate a fight there, or even that he was surprised. I mean a big hit like that. Had to be some blood, even small flecks laying around the shop. But it was clean, nothing."

"Alright, then. Someone didn't come to Henry. He came to them. Heard or saw something. Took the tool with him. Lost the fight. But there were no vehicle tire marks so was the assailant on foot? No sign of scuffle in the snow and dirt."

"No, sir. Nothing."

"Metal sweep was negative, correct?" the DS asked.

"Ah," the deputy knew the answer but looked anyway, pulling up the subfile from their site findings. "Yep, no steel, aluminum… "

"Do me a favor. What carbon factor was dialed in?"

"The range was 1.2-3.2. Why?"

"Because, deputy," he punched some words into a web browser. "Those numbers pull back steel. Steel is an alloy of about 1% carbon, mated with… "

He swiveled the screen.

Front Range Tool and Dye - 24 by 3/4 reversible ratchet in black. MSRP $144.50

"Iron. Get those detectors recalibrated, now."

It took forty minutes to get back onsite.

Late morning sunshine aided their quest. Four deputies spread out over the original evidence field. Sweeping patterns overlapped at their edges but otherwise they were covering their own quadrants. Every fifteen minutes they would switch. Rotating clockwise got them one full search grid four times over by noon.

"Nothing?"

"Yeah, sir. Nothing."

"Alright. Let's pack 'em up. It's cold. You guys are hungry. Shift change soon, too."

The DS turned toward the embankment, frustration coming out in his choice of words.

"Sarge?"

He turned back.

"Hey, Sarge. Everybody's good. Can we keep going? Don't even care about the OT if that's the problem. We all got a look at what happened down here. Another hour? Maybe two?"

The expanded grid led further into the woods.

The team began ascending the opposite hillside. A fenceline ranged across it. A few steps and sweeps more and they paused. Private property. Signs reaffirmed that basic right. A deputy worked his sensor right up against the split rail. And then slid it under and through. Signal and tone told the story.

"Hey!"

They all turned.

"Hey, I got something here!"

Three other deputies ran over, joined by the DS, and all thinking the same thing.

"Warrant?" the younger man asked.

The DS gave it only a second of thought. "I'd say we have the 'strong possibility of evidence pertaining to the commission of a crime, wouldn't you?'" The recitation, straight from county code, met nods all around.

"Besides," the DS smiled "we definitely can't pay the OT needed for you guys to hang around while we get a judge to sign off. It's nearly post-lunch naptime and we wouldn't get them up until at least two-thirty." The caricature was patently untrue, revealing a level of reasonably innocent inter-branch contention only resolved at the July Fourth County Games.

"Sir?"

"Deputy, you may proceed."

The junior officer slid through the fence and swept the immediate area. More tone, even stronger. A little to his left. Stronger still. He dropped the detector and knelt, pawing at the icy surface. A small hole opened. His gloved hand hit something harder than snow.

He stopped.

The DS stepped through the fenceline and with extra care brushed more snow from the edges of the hole, leaving the discovery in place as he dug around it.

The tool was dark black and looked to be two feet in length.

"Lab says about fifteen."

They'd raced back, cutting their return time to thirty-two minutes.

The five stood, pacing, wanting so much for this to be a break. The DS tried to busy himself with the beginnings of a report, especially the wording around the warrantless search of private property. He knew it wouldn't matter so much if they uncovered a rock-solid chain of evidence. Still, it had been a risk.

"Sarge," a deputy looked over, seeing the mental calculations. "Did the right thing out there. We'll all back you up. This is it, I can feel it. Whoever did this is on borrowed time, now."

The notification came up. Labs available.

Blood and hair were a match. The tool had been cleaned but held small amounts of physical evidence at the socket end. Blunt force imprint was less conclusive but in the range of "highly probable."

"Sorry, Henry," the DS breathed. "You didn't deserve any of this."

He scanned further down the report.

Tool handle cleaned. Partial print.

His heart sped.

A nice little pie chart graphic showed that the print was being processed. That was federal. Regardless of the reason, every single fingerprint file was kept in the Integrated Automated Fingerprint ID System. The FBI administered IAFIS. Seventy million criminal backgrounds with another few million from people who had actually gone to their community resource officer at some point locally to volunteer their prints and trusting they'd be used only for the common good.

The system was very fast. Still, they only had a partial.

"Okay," the DS waited. "We know *what*. I'd be very, very glad for some direction on *who*."

The circle went from one-third orange to all green.

The DS clicked the federal report link.

Townsend, Perry A.

Thirty-two years of age. Resident of Kittredge, Colorado.

A long list of petty theft and drug-related charges. At least until about three years ago, where the rap sheet ended abruptly.

"Huh," a deputy overlooked the DS's screen. "Got clean? Got religion?"

"Clean? Could be," the DS murmured. "Religion? If so, his articles of faith don't seem to include commandment number six. Deputy," he nodded. "Call in that warrant. We're going to Kittredge. Now."

TWENTY SIX

"And it's here we see the sinews, the systemic connectors."

The Brown professor had been holding their attention for ninety-five minutes. The side room on the third level of CHI Health Arena hosted only thirty for the exclusive pre-conference talk. Ten similar rooms held the same, each a different topic.

Weighing the cost of justice.

Poverty and the Environment.

Decolonizing Justice.

Criminal Justice Reform and the Death Penalty.

Taking Action Against the Injustice of Climate Change.

And others.

Ben was so glad to be in the room. The normal cost for these talks wasn't in an average grad student's budget. Twenty-eight seats had been sold at full price. Only then had Dr. Paulsen offered it to the team.

The speaker closed his prepared remarks and opened it up for Q&A.

"First, off, professor," a voice from up front. "It is so refreshing to see your work gaining a broader reach. I have pre-ordered your book and can't wait for it to come out."

The speaker smiled. "Well, thank you. That's quite kind."

"So, my question pertains to where we go from here. If more people understood the underpinnings and pervasiveness of the white power structure, we'd win the day, correct? So, what's the plan?"

"Ah, sounds like you want a conspiracy," he joked.

The questioner laughed. "Frankly, I'd love one. Anytime now."

"So, no, there's not a grand plan set into motion by the underbelly of a shadow government. This is all about evolution. Just like survival skills, ideas flourish or perish. If humanity has held stubbornly to ideas that keep us from flourishing, then we are duty-bound, for the survival of our species, to dismantle them, however and whenever they hold sway. We talk. We write. We perform," he nodded to a well-known musician in the third row, gracing their gathering as both activist and entertainer. "But we also act. We act with clarity and purpose. Government, politics, yes. Law enforcement. Social and community services. Religious and cultural institutions.

Now, are these entities all tied together at the head by some small cabal of leaders, meeting triannually in Geneva, or some other new world order location? No. That's ridiculous. We're aiming for a moment where the weight of humanity sees the value of progress. But, as I have laid out for you today, and — shameless plug — in my book… "

More laughter.

"Well, even a tenured faculty salary at Brown isn't what you'd think… "

The professor held court through another set of questions and then got the signal from the back of the room. One finger up.

"So, maybe one last question. It's been wonderful. Anyone?"

Ben weighed the opportunity. Was it relevant? Might as well. When would he have another chance like this?

The professor caught Ben's hand, cautiously rising in the back.

"First, I want to say thank you again. It's been a wonderful session with so much to think about."

"I sense a 'but'… coming… Ben, isn't it?"

Ben was surprised. They'd only shaken hands in a brief greeting.

"Ah, yeah. Ben. So, it's not a 'but,' just an honest question. Something I encounter in conversations and have been wondering about."

This one felt a bit more involved than the professor was hoping. He wanted something to pivot on, make a statement, and pitch the book one more time.

Ben continued. "So, I have some friends. Great people. Maybe a little different politically but great, caring people. They're willing to hear me out when I try to help them understand the underlying, systemic and structural pieces of race, power, and injustices of all kinds."

"And then they… " the professor led.

"Well, they want some actual data. More specifically, they want crime data. In their minds, and can't say I disagree, our progressive agenda has a lot to do with law and enforcement of ideals across society. If that's the case, they reason, we usually pass laws to address failures that are observable, you know, prosecutable. Because, again using their argument, laws are meant to curb undesirable behavior. I find it difficult to quantify the problem for them, at least in ways that would naturally suggest the remedies we most often put forward."

"So, your 'friends'… they don't believe that systemic racism exists?"

"No. I don't think that's quite right. They sort of hand me that as a willing presupposition."

"Ben. You're a graduate student in Social Justice at Creighton, correct? Maybe pre-law? You've likely read at least half of the literature out there on the subject. I summarized much of it only forty-five minutes ago. In my opinion, it's overwhelming. And I would say that very often people don't see what they don't want to see. And your friends must understand that this is not that kind of science. You expect math and chemistry, maybe engineering here?"

"No. I find what I am studying utterly compelling. At times, disturbing. Respectfully, I think they're just wanting a little more hard data to go with the survey and anecdotal work. And, I think if we could supply it, we'd win over many of similar opinion."

"Call me a cynic, Ben. But I think most people in your friends' position are simply looking for excuses to not make the changes they know are required to bring about a more just society. They like their privilege. Their position. And they've never for one moment had to live any other way. They seem kind but it's much the same kindness that acts one way in polite society while knowing full well they would never give away what they have. And that, Ben, is power. They use what they have to keep what they have. In this case, it's intellect. They may cede the basic principle but will filibuster any real acknowledgment of its depth and certainly not allow the conversation to move forward into real action."

Ben's mouth opened but the professor stepped from behind the small lectern and headed out to the book table.

"Thank you again," he said in the doorway. "I am very much looking forward to the conference."

"Nice work, Ben," Terri walked past.

Ben shrugged and looked her direction.

One hour later an email landed in a secure inbox.

The recipient was working from home and clicked "open."

Pre-conference finished. Security uneventful. Special guest confirmed with more details later today.

The man smiled, shut down the secure mail app, and closed the laptop cover. He walked downstairs slowly over deeply padded carpet. Through the hallway he turned left and then down a few stairs into the sunken great room. Mid-day on the mountain was astounding, even--maybe especially--in winter. Vast, undisturbed blankets of snow led to dark green pines. Standing resolute, these forests were the product of trial. Their selection was a result of a slow, careful refining and now they took their rightful place, unmoving, unmatched.

Often, he thought, men took their cues from nature. But yes, we so often over-complicate. All the while the patterns, the way forward, lay all around. Look. Observe. Learn.

There is an order to things. Keep that order and all is well. Harmony.

It was all so glorious.

TWENTY SEVEN

Carter was pretty happy with the day so far.

The fun day at the church had gone way better than anticipated. He needed that time with Mia and Theo far more than he realized. All three had enjoyed themselves. Mia was maturing faster than he'd like but she was still a great big sister. Even after finding a few friends from school, she made sure to keep an eye toward Theo. The inflatables were awesome. Everybody took a turn at the craft tables. They even made something for Mae, though a little time to herself was probably the best gift she could have received.

Carter found himself relaxed at lunch, the soup and company warming him thoroughly. They sat next to a very nice family while they ate. Small talk, totally normal. They were regular attenders but had only been coming for about a year. Had great things to say about the music, preaching, youth group, and kids programs. Carter's cynical head voice jumped forward but he caught it before it could finish the thought. Something about everything always looking great on the outside.

As he glanced around the multipurpose room he only saw happy people. At least, as best he could tell. He knew there were deep hurts, disappointments, serious questions seated at these tables. Experience and statistics told him that much. But he also got the sense that they weren't really trying all that hard to hide it. There was something genuine about the conversations, their facial expressions. He guessed most of these folks had found a church home here. And that they'd also found a way to both walk through hard things as well as enjoy good moments. As a pastor, he'd always wanted that for his congregation. Wasn't that a true mark of community?

On reflection, the only awkward moment was when he had been a little too aggressive with the archery tag. The music director was a good sport but the bruise surely forming on his back left thigh would linger at least a week. Carter's apologies came fast and repeatedly.

He dropped the kids back home with Theo and Mia giving an excited report to their mom before they even had their big coats off. Carter turned to Mae. Would she mind if he went in for a quick workout at District? They had a great, small gym.

Yep, no I know it's my day off. Promise I won't get pulled into anything.

Just be back in a couple hours, okay?

"I got next."

Carter looked up from the small bench along the wall. District 3 had a half-court outfitted with a nice acrylic backboard and even a three point line. Intending to spend some quality time with the free weights, he'd been pulled into three one-on-ones in a row. None had been much of a challenge. He was the next-oldest trooper at thirteen next to the shift sergeant. But the advanced of years rookie also had four years of small college hoops under his belt. In this case, sheer youthfulness was unable to overcome experience and skill. At least so far.

"Bradford," Carter noted, as she unzipped her hoodie and laid it aside.

"Yeah, been watching. Not bad. But these guys aren't gonna give you a run."

Carter knew something was up.

"Oh yeah, Jons," one of his vanquished foes spoke. "You didn't know? Bradford here was D1. Georgetown."

Carter glanced over as she began warming up. "Of course she was."

He put his hands on his knees, rose, and stepped out to meet her.

"Ten by ones?" he offered. "Threes are two?"

"Uh huh. Make it take it." She checked the ball to him. "Small college goes first."

"So very kind of you."

Carter took a hard step forward and left, pulled back quickly, separated and then shot over her too-far-away hands. It banked cleanly in.

"Oh my, one zip!" came from the guys. "But c'mon, Jons. You gotta call that bank next time."

Bradford ignored it, knew he'd meant to use the board. That wasn't luck. That was a shot he'd made thousands of times before.

She checked the ball back to him.

Carter moved the same way again, but this time he upper body faked the jumper and took one more step forward. She picked him clean, not even a small hand check. Faster than he would have imagined she sped back and over the three point line with the ball. He turned for defense as she switched from right to left, dribbling easily past and then stepping back into one of the smoothest shots he'd ever seen.

One-one.

He grabbed the ball as it fell through the net then checked it back out to her, waiting past the line. He could see the wheels turning. She'd sized him up in a sum total of two points. Now all she had to do was work her game plan.

Two more mid-range jumpers got her to three-one. A standing three got her to five-one. He barely saw the ball leave her hand the motion was so fast. Make it take it could be brutal. He needed to get possession or this was going to be over real quick.

She faked right and led left. Carter reached in and got a small piece of her wrist as she shot. He turned and blocked her out as the ball fell short, just kissing the rim. Neither of them was going to call a foul on that. Just part of the deal with good players.

Jons had the ball back. He faked hard from the three-line and she bit. He knew she'd be on him and went under for a reverse layup, just beyond her fingertips. Five-two. He was breathing harder than he'd intended for this quick mid-day workout. Still, it felt good. All senses were firing now, moving smoothly, on command.

Bradford seemed surprised he had another gear.

Carter hit a contested three. She was so close to sending that one back into his face.

Five-four.

Then something changed in her countenance. She was breathing even heavier but not out of exhaustion. She was getting angry. She swiped the ball from him again, this time with a bit of body as he tried to turn the corner toward the basket. Again, neither were going to call that one. Bradford had had enough. Two more lightning fast threes and then a single pivot move from the bottom right post.

Ten-Four.

"Oh, oh, oh!" came the call from the sidelines. "Winner and still undefeated champ*een*."

She grabbed her gear and walked off. Not a word.

"Hey, Jons," the shift sergeant approached. "Don't feel so bad."

"Ah, sarge, were we watching the same game?" he swallowed hard, catching his breath. "That was pretty ugly. Like she was just playing with me. I've seen cats show more interest as they swat away their mostly-dead prey."

"Yeah, that's not a bad image. But I don't think so."

Carter didn't get it.

"No one has ever even *scored* on her, Jons. Four points must burn pretty deep."

"Seems like a lot about her burns pretty deep."

"For good reason."

Again, Carter wasn't following.

"Look, it's not the whole story, for sure. But… " he lowered his voice just a little. "Pleasanton. Arkansas. 1952. Look it up when you have a minute. Might not be bad to get to know your fellow trooper a bit more."

TWENTY EIGHT

The paved driveway led a half mile up the mountain.

The detective sergeant drummed mindlessly on the steering wheel. His eyes were drawn upward, into the massive pines, forming a tunnel the last three hundred yards. Once out, he pulled into the large circular drive.

Nice place.

He got out, closed the door, and headed for the front entrance. Twelve beautifully hewn stone steps led up to the video bell. The DS paused and turned. The view back out from the house brought a low whistle from him.

"Hello," an attractive woman greeted. "Oh, officer?"

"Yes, ma'am. Jefferson County Sheriff's office," he produced his badge. "We're investigating a probable homicide. Terrible thing."

"Oh my," she stepped back. "What? Near here?"

"Well, actually, no. Idledale. But... " he looked into the open door. "Your husband? Is he in this afternoon? We called the head office and then the mill. They said he might be working from... "

"Dear?" came a question from behind her. A man stepped forward.

"Sir," the DS repeated, "very sorry to disrupt your day but I am from the Jefferson County Sheriff. We're following up on some information on an employee of yours."

The man nodded.

"Your mill manager said he'd be glad to cooperate but felt you should be in the loop." He looked back again toward the pines. "Amazing spot you've got here."

"Well, thank you," the man said. "Yes, we love it. Please, please do come in" he shifted tone. "A bit cold to talk on the front steps this time of year."

"Okay," the DS blew into his hands. "That would be wonderful. Thanks."

The wife opened the door fully and then shut it behind them.

"Wow," the DS nodded toward the great room. "Another horrible view."

"Ha, yes. How about the library. Just this way. Dear?" he asked, "I was just finishing up some tea." He turned to the officer. "Tea, deputy?"

"Oh, sure. That would be great. And not that it matters, but… it's 'sergeant.' It gets confusing at times with a sheriff's office. Seems like everybody should just be a deputy, which technically we are. But my focus area is investigation, so I am actually a detective sergeant."

"Certainly… *sergeant*. And thank you, dear…" he directed to his wife as she headed to the kitchen. He turned back to his guest. "What would you like to know?"

The DS pulled out a small pad of paper. He knew it was cliche. Still, worked just fine, even after all these years.

"Perry Townsend. He works in your finish room?"

"Yes, he does," alarm crept forward. "He's got a great eye for detail. Important for the millwork pieces we produce for finish carpentry. Perry's been a fine addition to our team. Hard worker. Given his past, we're especially proud of him."

"Ah, thanks for mentioning that. He has not had an easy road of it from his criminal record it seems."

"No, not easy at all. His background is quite tragic. But we've seen such a change in him these last few years. Grown close. We try and keep things that way, you know. More than just a job. Such a rich heritage we've been given. Try to do our bit at honoring the past and building on it. Employees like Perry, well, they're more like... family."

The DS was scribbling while he listened. "That's great. Really great. So, Perry called in sick yesterday, Wednesday. That's correct?"

"I was unaware of the reason, but yes, I didn't see him yesterday, now that I think of it."

The man's eyes begged for clarification.

"I don't want to be overdramatic here, sir, — and forgive me my bluntness--but just six hours ago a deceased male was found in a ravine outside Idledale."

The man gasped. "No... Perry?"

"No, sir," he noted the response. "The deceased was a local... machine shop owner. But we've located the weapon. And we have a confirmed print."

The man gasped a second time.

"Sergeant... that can't be. That simply can't be."

"Forensics on this are both local and from the Bureau. Unless he's got a really, really good reason for the prints, Perry is our alleged. We need to know anything we can about where he might be, why he would have done something like this. Like you said, given the good trajectory he's been on."

The man looked down and composed himself.

"I am glad to help. Really, sergeant. In any way. But I cannot imagine Perry doing something like this. I just can't... it makes no sense. Why he'd even begun dating recently."

"Okay, so let's go there. Name and contact info? Anything?"

He wrote some more notes.

"I know this is difficult," he continued. "But, Perry's world for most of his adult life was in the shadows, with pretty dark people, and the appetites that go along with it."

"You mean the drugs?"

"Yes. Is there any chance he had begun using again? Maybe even selling? Work checked out? Nothing to note there?"

"Why no. Nothing at all. Like I said he was one of our most valuable employees."

The DS noted the shift in reference.

"Okay, so this new relationship. Still together? No reason for a setback? No one else that you know of that would complicate things?" The machine shop owner was an unlikely love challenge but could it be that he was related somehow? A disapproving relative? That would be easy enough to check out.

"Sergeant. This is all so sudden. But, no. I'd just heard things were going really well."

The DS sighed and closed his notebook. He stood just as the wife entered. "Oh, thanks so much but we're done for now. Appreciate everything."

"At least take a cookie, deputy," she offered.

He smiled without correcting, grabbed the sweet, and headed to the front door.

"Thank you, again."

The DS got back into his car and headed down the mountain.

"Call office," he said, leaning toward his phone in its cradle.

"Hey, Sarge."

"Heading back from the mill owner interview. Couple of immediate follow ups on Townsend. He's got a girl," he heard typing on the other end.

"Got it. We'll get on it, sarge. Hey, you get back to the Bureau yet?"

The DS tapped his screen. Five messages. Same number.

"Uh, no but I am guessing this is him."

"Probably, but it's a her."

"Ah, yeah. Ok. Anything from Townsend's apartment. Those couple of boxes?"

"Sorting through them and should be finished by the time you get back."

"Got it. Back in fifteen."

He hung up the call and pressed the number on the last of the five messages. Sixty seconds later his concern level, already heightened, went through the roof.

"… we've been watching them for about a year, now," came from the other end. "So far, though, all talk, no action. But then the prints pull came through and it pinged my file."

The DS sped up as he listened.

"Sergeant," the fed got it right. "You need to find this guy. If not, we're just waiting for something very bad to happen. The people he's been associating with the last three years? We're gonna all wish they were small time druggies. I'm running a threat-level assessment request up the chain."

"That feels a little heavy."

"Not if you knew what I know, sergeant. You've got a head start there. Given his last known position at Idledale and the winter weather in the passes, I think we're looking east, the greater plains region. Denver to Chicago. Kansas City up to the Dakotas. You have to narrow that down for us. We need to know where

Townsend is headed. Your murder case is not just local anymore."

Townsend's phone buzzed four times. The dark web app did its job and then disappeared without even so much as an icon on screen.

He should have been alarmed.

But it had been an exhausting last thirty-four hours and he was sleeping heavily, the phone muffled by a knit cap in his coat pocket in the small hotel room closet.

TWENTY NINE

Carter's jaw kept dropping.

The more he found, the worse it got. He literally felt sick to his stomach.

He'd not been gone long for the workout, just as promised. Home by 2:30, he gave Mae a "See, I know how to tell time" look, to which she replied with a golf clap. He'd mentioned the three games he'd won. Bradford's victory, notably, was not brought up. Over the next two hours he checked some items off the home list. Four inches of fresh snow needed to be blown out of the driveway. He'd long ago switched from shoveling as the primary mode of removal. Still, it took a certain amount of skill, a plan actually, to get the white stuff out of the way and not have it come back at you. Carter mouthed to himself that this was not his mess to clean up.

Overheard as he stepped back inside, Mae reminded him: neither were diapers.

"Dinner at 6," she notified.

He'd walked upstairs imagining her enchiladas.

Now he wasn't so sure he could eat.

The accounts were horrendous. Reality was worse.

Spring 1952- Pleasanton, Arkansas.

Four young men took turns striking the black teen.

"You oughta know better."

Another blow.

"Maybe you're not so smart, huh?" one held the now-crumpled report card. "Because if you were smarter, you'd know your place. Why do think you need all that book learnin' anyways? Gonna be somebody? Somethin' important? No you ain't!"

More blows. The teen could no longer stand. He had long since stopped crying, was nearly unconscious, limp. His pleas for mercy fell on not just deaf, but cruel, ears.

"You know what I think of your smarts? Here's what I think… " the larger boy threw the paper down on the ground, relieving himself on it.

One more punch and the two boys holding him let go. He fell, hard, no hands out to stop it. They kicked him in the ribs. Each one took a turn. The boy didn't move.

"Somebody's comin!"

"Leave him."

"But, what if he's dead?"

"What about it? You think the sheriff's son and his friends are gonna get nailed for this? For *him*?"

Antiochus Bradford survived that day. His wounds took time to heal. Especially the wounds of heart and mind. Still, the boy knew — contrary to his attackers' claims — he'd been put here for something important. He only studied harder. Took every opportunity afforded him, even as roadblock after roadblock stood in his way. Decades later he wore the badge that had failed him so horribly as Sheriff of Pleasanton, AR.

The call came in after midnight.

Sheriff Bradford headed out, already knowing the parties involved. On arrival he talked his way into the small home, words perhaps the most well-honed tool in his arsenal. Past the front entry, he eased his way back and then through the kitchen.

Eyes bloodshot, hair up but tangled, the woman's face played out a mix of fear and anger. The gun in her hand wavered between Antiochus and the other man, three feet away at the edge of the deep shag carpet.

"I *will* do it," she seethed. "He's got it comin'. See my arms?" she moved her shoulder. Deep black finger marks came into view.

"No, you don't want to do this. Miss, you really don't," Antiochus calmed.

"Yeah, baby," the man added. "C'mon now. You know we just get out of hand sometimes."

"NO!" she aimed squarely at the man's face. "I am done with you. Evil! No other word for it. From the pit of Hell! Now I'm gonna send you where you belong. Where you can't hurt nobody else." She steadied, pulling back the hammer.

"Hey! Sheriff," backup had arrived and just heard the click of the gun.

"Easy, everybody easy, ok," Antiochus kept his hands where she could see them. "Deputy. Outside... " his voice was even but strong. "Just stay there."

Antiochus turned back.

It was all a blur of motion and passion.

The boyfriend lunged forward.

She let go.

The gun dropped.

The boyfriend stumbled, somehow catching the sidearm by its grip. His forward motion was too much and the weapon dropped to the floor.

A bang, a muzzle flash.

The woman looked to Antiochus, then fell forward, dead.

In that instant Sheriff Bradford noticed the gloves. Long, white gloves. And her dress. The scene became only more sickening. The boyfriend made her dress up and then decided she was undesirable, finding in her something worthy of the scars.

Antiochus drew down on the boyfriend, freezing him in place.

The deputies rushed the scene, now unholstered as well.

"Sheriff, you alright?" they moved to subdue the man, cuffed him.

"Wait!" the boyfriend screamed from the floor, face down and hands behind. "I didn't do it. You *know* I didn't. You were here the whole time! Do the right thing, s*heriff.*"

The boyfriend's prints were the only ones on the gun. Antiochus was the sole witness. He could have considered it vengeance, maybe even just. The universe bending in the direction of recompense.

Antiochus didn't even blink.

Instead, he told the truth. And so one of the boys pummeling Antiochus into blackness so many years ago received the fairness and respect he himself was never offered.

Carter was crying. He found it near impossible to focus his eyes on the rest of the wiki page.

But there was so much more than just the accounts of the man's near-deathly beating and his moment of truth, where who he was and what he'd been called to do on this planet was never more on display. When principled courage outweighed any desire for vengeance. That particular scene had long been kept silent, brought forward near the end of his life only when a documentary filmmaker friend of Amy's finally got him to reveal it. Amy was shocked. It was a stunning and powerful piece, the man's grit and honor its true stars.

The remainder of the elder Bradford's law enforcement career played out equally challenging and successful. Commendations. Advancements. Amid the whims of multiple mayoral administrations, many appreciating his steady hand while keeping him at arms' length socially, he kept advancing the cause of justice in places it had not seen the light of day for many generations. He was one of the first to welcome and set in motion DNA processing of crime scene evidence in his state. He never wavered from duty and the trust the people of Pleasanton repeatedly placed in him. At least enough of them come election time to keep the badge on his chest.

Antiochus Bradford's second son, Amy Bradford's father, excelled as well, a defense attorney by trade, continuing the family's presence in the halls of justice.

Carter wiped his eyes and dropped his head.

He knew he'd had no idea. Now he knew exactly how much he had no idea.

He and Amy had lived in the same country. A common constitution and sets of laws. Their socio-economic worlds were not completely foreign to one another. Middle-class. College educated. Carter had an extra few years of school in seminary but that was very specialized graduate work. So, he thought, how is it we can also have so profoundly different paths. No, not *different* paths. The same basic road. Same hills to get over in general, same downhill sides to coast. But maybe mine was reasonably paved and hers was more like gravel. Maybe mud. Slower. Harder. Plenty of temptation to give up, and with good reason.

His shift sergeant's words came back: "You know she's a *person*, right?"

Carter let them settle, even deeper this time.

THIRTY

"You see how I'm doing it? Get busy on your load."

Townsend had been watching closely the last thirty minutes. Layering the material into the ribbed plastic wire track required finesse. Using a large funnel he poured the contents in, two linear feet at a time. Once he'd completed ten fillings, he'd pack the dirty clay-like substance with a hand trowel, the kind you'd use in your backyard garden. A simple two-wire detonation run would go from end to end with a plastic connector end cap, hidden among a regular bundle of cat5 and coax. These finished twenty-foot-long sections were their building blocks. Placed evenly under the arenas Level 100 subflooring, they'd blend in with the other miles of cabling required to make a place like CHI Health Center run. Best of all, Richards knew, chemical sensors currently in service by law enforcement would find nothing of concern. Even upon close inspection, the story of inexpensive, and again eco-friendly, insulation would win the day.

Each truck carried enough material to make the track runs. Twenty for the device and spares. Connected end to end from Section 101 through 110 and then again 116 through 125, the succession of blows would build with maximum blast achieved at the 80% point of each run. The resulting overpressure would overwhelm the structure. Level Two would fail instantly. Then the roof would simply collapse. A third of the attendees had floor seats. The remainder would occupy the two levels on the sides. This was as thorough destruction as Richards could guarantee with the materials they could get in place unnoticed and on the desired schedule. But there were six full seating sections on both levels the blast would not reach--the far ends of the arena. While total destruction would have been preferable, this would more than do the trick.

"You'd better pick it up," Richards said. "I'm not doing your work. Do the math, kid. At thirty minutes apiece, you're barely gonna make the schedule."

"I'm getting faster. But this stuff doesn't pour so easy."

"All the better for enhanced catalytic activity."

"What?"

"Nevermind. You just need twenty good sections done by 6am. We clean up and leave by 7. If I have to leave you here, I will. Not my problem. I still get paid."

That part about leaving him here landed ominously.

Townsend focused on his work. It wasn't unlike the finish mold room at the mill.

He found a groove and began packing almost rhythmically. Earbuds in, he worked more and more efficiently, enjoying his favorite podcasts and almost glowing with purpose. Since being welcome in by *The Family* he'd been impressed with their care, their concern, and their zeal. Not to mention they were successful. He wanted that as well. Business. Money. Family. Really hoped this would be the start of something wonderful for him. His new girlfriend seemed the kind of woman to grow old with. What a turnaround that would be. From suicidal addict to community leader and family man. Someone worth something. Someone worthy.

Perry marveled at the mission scope.

As far as he knew — and he was correct — *The Family* was not connected to some greater network. How they'd come across Richards was a good question, but on the whole they were a small group from the western suburbs of Denver and that was it. He'd wondered about further allegiances but was told, and he believed them, that the only worthwhile actions were local actions. Again, this apparent contradiction — Omaha was not their community — was satisfied with further context. The system as it was was so thoroughly entangled with deep money that you could never rely on anything at the national, maybe not even the state level. It also made a certain kind of sense. Even his limited understanding of history led him to believe that America was at her best as a collection of individual communities, linked by a basic and binding set of agreements. It was a big country. Plenty of room for everyone. As long as they kept to themselves and didn't try and enforce their norms on other people, other places. Perry didn't want to be part of a movement per se. He just wanted family.

So, their impact would be outsized. Hopefully it would spur similar localized actions. Enough to at least halt the crazy. Enough to put a pause on the forces that had seemed to gain so much momentum the last few years. Thinking back to his youth, it was difficult to recognize the country he'd grown up in. With rare exception, the very things he should be able to count on had begun to spiral. There were new rules. New offenses all the time. Most offputting was the policing even of language. It maddened him.

"You have no right," he grumbled, loud enough for Richards to look over from his workstation.

Realizing he had let that out, he nodded and got back to his work.

Perry stopped as he finished a section. He'd just popped the end-connector in place and counted "three" to himself. It was going to be a long night. But at the end? He had the opportunity to be a part of something very special.

The three men gathered again in the great room. The mountain was darkening.

"Nothing?"

"No, but I am not surprised. We were communication silent."

"How could he be so stupid?" the third one entered the conversation.

"I thought he was coming along. Working hard. Staying clean. The girlfriend?"

"Yes, that's another issue altogether. How well do we know her? Her family?"

"Not well, unfortunately. Moved to town just a month ago. She followed her mother here. Some community college classes. Barrista. She and Perry hit it off. Couldn't stop talking about her at work."

The homeowner sat back, staring into the woods. "Well, we knew there would be contingencies. Every battle plan is useless once engagement begins. Gentlemen," he tossed back the remaining contents of a glass tumbler, "it's only a matter of time. Twenty-four hours. Good thing we secured experienced help, and… with a range of services, should we need them."

"Indeed."

"Agreed," the third man added. "But what about the first driver?"

"Justyn?"

"Yes. Won't we need 'services' for him, as well?"

"I hardly think so at this point. If he'd wanted to harm the operation we'd have known about it sooner. I am sure the young man has simply run. There's no chance of him pointing back at us if that was his response to fear in the first place."

While not said, all three wondered about the quality of those they'd entrusted with such responsibility.

"No," the man continued. "We'll not hear from him again. The young man in Omaha is our only outstanding liability."

"And that will be accounted for in a timely fashion?"

"Yes, within the hour."

Another forty-five minutes and Richards felt his phone buzz.

"Hey," he motioned toward Townsend.

"Yeah?" Perry looked over, reluctant to stop his work.

Hungry? Richards pantomimed.

Townsend nodded. He was moving through the pieces now but could use a quick bite.

Richards gave him a thumbs up, walking past the small bathroom in the storage unit and into a mostly empty front room with a single coffee table. He opened the deli bag and retrieved a sandwich for each of them. He also thumbed a quick reply on his phone via the dark web app.

With that, he'd just secured another half-million.

A little clean-up work after their install would be good for both himself and his employer.

He walked back out and handed Perry the sandwich.

"Thanks."

"You bet."

THIRTY ONE

Was that his Dad's face?

Justyn struggled to focus the vision. The cold was doing its job. So was dehydration. His air supply felt different. And now, for-real claustrophobia was beginning to settle. He had no idea if he was awake, asleep, alive, or dead.

Justyn…

Distorted as it was, it was unmistakably his father.

"Dad?…" he croaked. "Dad?…"

Why?…

"What… what," in hoarseness.

How could you do this? What monstrosity have you become?

Justyn wept. Wet streams stained his cheek. "I…", he stammered. "I only wanted… "

What? You wanted what?

"You… I only ever wanted you."

Justyn tried to shake it away.

Still, the images and experience were so palpable. The previous hell-horrors ending with the slam of a gavel in judgment. Now, his father's disappointment. He desperately wanted this all to be over. Justyn didn't believe he had heard from God. Or that he'd received a post-death return of his father to warn him. No, this was all chemicals and failing biology. He'd hated stories that used the fear of punishment to induce obedience. Scrooge was weak. Dante was a fool. But here he was, trying to fight back the understandable emotions brought on by both messages.

In a quick and painful moment of lucidity it all faded away.

The water had been piling up, freezing his toes, then his feet, and now was working its way up his legs. It would have been one thing if the first few inches numbed. Instead, every new segment of iced tissue cried out before the nerve endings gave way. It was excruciating.

"Ahhhhhhhh!" Justyn yelled, still unable to move his torso. "No. Nnnnnn.... NO!"

He breathed quicker, trying to control the pain. He had no feasible means of shortening his demise. It would come when it would come. And every indication showed it would come slowly at this point. Slowly and agonizingly.

He tried to shake off the pain and the impending deeper thoughts.

Both gripped Justyn violently.

Heaven had always been a mystery to him. If it was all harps and togas, then forget it. Who would want to live a restrictive life, only to be met with endless boredom and *that* sound. Justyn had no idea the Bible painted the end like it painted the beginning. That the perfection the first two humans had been invited into started in a garden but was meant to have that garden-state expand to fill the entire world. Bodies, minds, relationships all set in motion to explore, to create, to understand. To unpack the incredibly wondrous gift that an immeasurably good and powerful God had set before them. To know and unravel mysteries of physics, biology, engineering, technology still too far in the future for modern man to grasp. And to do this all under the watchful and good eye of their creator. What was made perfect was intended to continue that way, just more so.

Justyn had no idea the very strife that so chafed between races was a non-issue in eternity. Hadn't even begun to think that one through. And a vision of all nations, tribes, and tongues gathered under and guided by this same God forever? Not even on his furthest mental horizon. Everything in his world was broken. And so it made perfect sense his understanding of the ultimate good was, as well. It just was terribly tragic no one had ever disabused him of such untruth.

And what of hell?

Justyn had that equally wrong. As caricatured as heaven, it brought no lasting sense of danger. First off, he was reasonably assured of the other option on the basic merits of a generic faith of good deeds, where good was defined by the voices closest around him. He didn't like what he thought of heaven. Still, if forced to wager he felt solid about his chances. But, what if he were not on the good list? What if hell was his destination on the other side of the grave. Well, he and his friends assured themselves they'd all be there together. One big party. That's what Satan liked to do, right? Seems like everything fun in life always had the devil attached to it. So, why wouldn't he just spit in God's eye for *literally ever* by inviting the people who said no thanks to the sissy dress and pearly gates and opted instead for one, massive, endless frat party?

That's what Justyn had thought. As the pain surged through his calves, he regained a small bit of that belief. But his mental state was slipping and the recent hallucinations shook him. Quite hard, actually. Not so much his ideas about heaven.

But, what of hell?

What if the devil wasn't in control there? What if he also was there under someone else's rule? Someone else's judgment. If so,

Justyn would face the same.

And that was what Justyn still felt, lingering, brooding, challenging.

He felt judgment.

Wrath.

A giant cracking exploded in his ears.

Justyn's body twisted to the right. His upper body rotated with the force of gravity.

His legs did not.

He heard the snapping.

Then pain, unlike he'd felt before, shot through his shins and up through his knees.

He screamed again.

"Ahhhhhhhhhhh. Uhhhh. Pleeeeeeease," he cried out. "What more do you want?!!!"

While his brain had not been working very well as of late, it definitely still knew how to produce endorphins.

Justyn got angry.

"I've done what I've done! You were never there anyway! I had to figure it out on my own. Don't like it? Maybe you could have sent someone my way to help! What? You're supposed to be *good*? What's good about taking away someone's dad? What's good about leaving me to struggle and never know it's good enough? If you *are* in charge, I don't want to live that way forever. I couldn't trust you before… "

The sound of water gathered at his feet.

Another inch came in through the breached windshield.

Justyn felt it freezing rather quickly.

When he stopped shouting, he realized he was spent. He also realized the van had shifted yet one more time. And while he now had a compound fracture, he also had an enormous eight inches of room about his head, shoulders, and even one arm. He rotated and brought his right hand up, past his waist, along his side, and then up near his cheek.

His skin was patchy, rough. His eyes drooped. His hand fell back down at his side, just slightly to the right of where they had been the many hours before. Once there his pinky brushed against his phone, previously out of reach. He moved his fingers and felt a cable, and then at the end of the cable, another small block.

The charger.

While the heat pouch had been playing out he'd hooked up his phone, one last charge for whatever time he had remaining, even though at the time he still had no reception. It should have zeroed out by now. But the cold had slowed the charge, taking instead the several hours he lay immobilized to reach full. Now, as he lifted it, he saw it was at 100%.

And there, at the far right top of the screen: a single bar of signal strength.

THIRTY TWO

Carter was catching a few more minutes in his home office.

He'd managed to eat dinner. Still, he felt nauseous, unsettled.

The revelations of Pleasanton held on like a bad headache. He struggled to even begin to process the kind of hatred he'd read about. But that was it, really. He'd only had to read it. Had never experienced anything like it. Not remotely. His chances of encountering significant levels of danger, threat, or even harassment due to his skin tone were as close to zero as you could get. Day after day, he had walked in the, well, privileges, of majority status as a given. He didn't like the hammer the term had become, but there was no denying it. Why, he thought, would you deny something that's demonstrably true, a basic part of social reality? The question to him wasn't whether or not he had privilege. Instead, what had he done—and what was he now—doing with it? It wasn't sin. He'd had no choice in the matter. But Bradford's grandpa's story had disrupted his heart, positively so.

It also angered him.

What in the world had made them so cruel, so thoughtless, so ugly? Honestly, he wished he had been around for teen Antiochus' encounter with evil. He was sure he'd have fought for him. No amount of historical displacement could convince him otherwise.

He knew his heart. Knew he would act. Whether or not they would have carried the day, given the time and locals' thinking, was another question. But no, put me in a time capsule, land me three minutes before those...

He caught his words. *Choice words*, his mom used to say.

"We may not have won the war but that battle would've been ours, for sure," he mumbled.

Carter grabbed the stack of opened envelopes at the right edge of his desk. He could pay a couple bills real quick before the kids were done with baths. He could hear Mae and Theo laughing and splashing. Mom had a plastic shark coming at him from under the bubbles. Every few seconds an "attack" was followed by a squeal and then a chuckle from both.

"Ok. Who gets money this week?" Carter joked. "House. You're good until the 15th. Electric - uh, maybe. Strong contender, especially since it's winter. Hey there? What are you... "

Carter had one envelope still sealed.

Thomas Beckins, Attorney at Law.

He opened it, scanned it. His countenance dropped. The normal monthly installment had jumped dramatically. Almost doubled.

"That can't be right."

Carter looked to the *new charges* line on the invoice.

Roth - Moral Failure Defense. Billed hours. Pre-trial. Investigation. Beckins' notes clarified the full cost. The pre-trial settlement from the church covered only half. His lawyer thought it likely as good a deal they were going to get unless pressing it forward. Of course they wanted to settle. As quickly as possible. But still, there were more than five-thousand dollars there that had not been before.

Carter found it impossible to focus.

"All off at Sleepytown… " Theo tried to help, waiting for his dad to utter the rehearsed lines so he could fall off his back and onto the soft bedding.

"Oh, yeah. Sorry bud. Yes, allllllll off at Sleepytown."

Theo landed with another laugh.

"Hey, bud. Let's get you under those covers," Carter meandered.

"Ah," Theo let out a sigh as he snuggled in.

Carter's mind wandered even more.

Five thousand?

Why was he shocked. *Carter you idiot*. Never got to trial so there's no 'win' to take fees from. It was a settlement. And unless you want to drag everyone through that horror show, including… Jenny…

"Daddy… "

"Oh, yep. Theo, hey, you look real tired, son. That's good, just close those eyes."

A big yawn, even for a three-year-old.

Carter's head began spinning even more. He couldn't shake it. Just one more gut punch. One he should have seen coming. It was unbelievable. How in the world was he going to afford that? All because of those sneaky, smarmy, power-hungry little people. So small. Petty.

His angered roused and he imagined confrontations with them instead of Antiochus' foes. He was winning, every single time.

"Daaaaa… " Theo mouthed from near-sleep. It was quiet. Serene. A trusted title, even from the edges of consciousness. Effortlessly, Theo called out his father's name. Not in fear. In peace. Knowing he was present. Without any doubt whatsoever.

That can be you, too.

Carter paused. The impression held him the briefest second. Inaudible, yes. But clear. He let it sink in as he rose and moved to Mia's room.

"Sweetie. Time to shut it down. Another new book?"

"Yup."

"So, tell me the story."

Five full minutes later she brought it to a close. "… and the people the King thought were all fighting against him were not, really. There was another guy who just wanted to make it seem that way. Then they'd all be mad at each other and the Kingdom would fall, caput."

"*Caput*?"

"Yeah, you know. Caput."

"Okay. Caput."

"But the really sad thing," she reflected, "… is they fought a bunch of battles with each other before the bad guy's plan was found out."

Carter stared.

"Daddy?"

"Ah. Oh yeah. Nothing. That really is super sad, sweetie."

"It's okay. They finally figured it out."

"Yeah, Mia. Sounds like they did."

A fatherly kiss met her forehead as he brushed her hair away from her face.

Carter stepped out of the room and headed back to his study. He grabbed his worn Bible off the shelf and placed it just to the left of his keyboard.

"Father… "

Twenty minutes later he rose from his desk, having done significant heart-work before God. Like all such moments it was surrender, not victory. At least, not yet. Downstairs, he approached Mae, reading at their small breakfast table.

"Hey," he started.

"Babe,' she smiled, pulling off the readers she'd only recently given into.

"I don't want the Kingdom to fall."

She looked up.

"You know. Caput."

Mae cocked her head.

"Mia has a new word."

He paused. "And I want what Theo has."

"Legos and a giant stuffed bear?"

"Nice."

"Okay, serious. Translate."

"I can't keep doing this. The other night, when you said it was probably time to move on. You're so right. But, I gotta tell you this is the hardest thing I've ever had to face. I… I *hate* those people. I hate what they've done to us. And I know, I know. How many times have I preached on it? Hate is eating me up inside. It's killing me, not them. I know. It's so, so wrong. And it's not helping me become what I need to become now. Or what I still need to be for us, you, the kids. And my relationship with God. My faith. It's like it's all on autopilot. I can't do that anymore. I can't tell you I am healthy spiritually. But I want to be. And part of that is… well, a no-holds-barred trusting my good Father. And then, you know, trusting people who claim to follow Him."

"CJ… maybe you just need some more time. I mean, the church fun thing. That was great, right? Good steps?"

"Yeah, Mae. It was nice. But no, I don't need any more time. I've wasted enough already."

THIRTY THREE

"Jefferson County Sheriff. Hello, Miss? Miss? If you're here please open up. We have some questions about your boyfriend, Perry Townsend?"

They knocked a third time, just to be certain. Nightfall dropped the temperature again. The deputies' breath floated for a moment in the dim apartment stoop light. The visit corresponded with the end of her shift. She should be here. They'd already peered into the front room window as best they could. Nothing out of place. Seemed like it should if someone left for work and just hadn't gotten home yet.

"Okay, her workplace is how far?" one of them looked at his phone. "Maybe she made a quick grocery run on the way home. We'll circle back in another hour."

They headed east for only two and a half miles. Kittredge had a few main strips where commerce and life took place. There was even a quaint main street with as much history as you'd like, mixed in with rebuilds.

They stopped and got out.

Elevation Coffee has done well in its first few years of operation, situated right next to one of the oldest and few remaining Ben Franklin's in the country. Depending on your thinking, two armed deputies coming in right before close could offer a range of possibilities. They approached the counter.

"Hey. Get you guys something? It's cold out there. On the house, for sure."

This seemed the better of scenarios.

"Maybe on the way out, thanks. Appreciate it."

"Well, same. We're super glad for all you guys do around here. We're shutting down in just a few. Something we can help with?"

A woman stepped out of the small back office. "Yeah. What can we do for you guys?"

"We're trying to contact Candice. Candice Price? Had info that she worked here."

"Dee?"

"Is that what she goes by?"

"Yeah, hated the nickname 'Candy.' Especially with the last name 'Price.' So, shorten even more and you get 'Dee.'"

The deputy nodded in understanding and empathy.

The woman took another step forward. "Is she okay? Oh my gosh. Dee. She just left like an hour and a half ago."

"Ma'am. We tried her apartment and no one was there. Does she have a roommate by chance, someone else we can contact?"

"Ah, no. And that doesn't sound right. She hates driving out at night when it's like this. We try to close her shifts a little earlier but tonight we had some other staff call in sick. She would have gone right away. You're saying she's not there?"

"Well, it's certainly possible. Maybe she was in the shower or in the kitchen. But we knocked pretty loud and made sure anyone there knew we were present."

The other deputy stepped in. "So, no chance she would have just stopped by the store quick or something like that?"

"No. No," the man at the counter said. "My wife is right. She will not go out in this kind of weather unless absolutely necessary. How can we help? You've tried calling her, I assume."

"Correct" the first deputy answered. "And voicemail is full."

"Text?" the wife offered, but then shot down her own idea. "Um, yeah, I guess I wouldn't answer one that said it was the police either."

"Me, too," the deputy added. "Especially one with bad grammar, which," he joked, "my esteemed colleague here would for sure send."

"Have you tried Perry?"

The deputy tried to keep it straight. "We're definitely trying everything we can think of, right now."

"I don't suppose we could ask," the man probed. "Is Dee in trouble?"

"We're not at liberty to divulge anything at the moment but Dee is not currently suspected of any wrongdoing. She may have some information we desperately need."

"Wait," the woman interjected. "Her mom. Why didn't I think of that earlier?"

"Thanks, ma'am but we tried there as well. Mom headed back to where they moved from, had to close up some house sale items and such. Gone for the week."

All four paused, having run out the list.

"Anything else," the deputy began the close. "Anything at all? She seemed normal, at least for her? The last week or so? Nothing you noted?"

"Yeah, nothing I saw," the man answered. "You? Honey?"

The wife took a breath. "Well, I did think she was a little preoccupied Monday during her shift."

He seemed surprised.

"Dee never makes mistakes at the register. Two on Monday, in one shift. Asked if everything was okay. She was so embarrassed. Was it something with her new boyfriend? Her mom? She didn't say anything but I could just kinda tell. I let her know it was no big deal, gave her an extra long meal break."

Her husband had the *where was I this whole time?* look on his face.

"Well, thanks very much. We're headed back to her apartment in a bit. I'm sure everything will be okay," the deputy assured. "You can check back for any more info, or if you think of anything else." He handed over his card.

"Alright," the man replied. "Two to go? Let's keep you warm out there. What's your order?"

She set the phone down for the fifth time. With knees pulled up and fingers tugging slightly at her long hair, Candice Price tried to make it all go away.

Home directly after her shift, she had put some canned soup into a pot while she grabbed bread and lunchmeat from the cupboard and fridge. It was straightforward, and honestly, all the energy she had at the end of the day. Propping her phone up on the sugar container on the counter, she gasped at the news headline.

Idledale murder. Suspect on loose. Investigation in process. Jefferson County Sheriff seeking any and all information. And then the number to call.

Right next to Perry's face.

She ran. Poured the room temp soup down the drain. Took the sandwich. She backed out of the apartment driveway and then froze. Her terror doubled at the thought of heading out on the roads at this time of night, in these conditions. She didn't think through how this would look. She was innocent after all. Had nothing to do with whatever craziness Perry and that... family...

were up to. She really got the creeps from them. Perry was a good soul, at least one on the mend. The kind she'd always seemed to connect with. But them? No. She wanted nothing to do with what seemed to her a veneer. Fake. Something not quite right. A little Stepford. A little… well, she couldn't put her finger on it yet. But it had always bothered her. And now she wanted nothing at all to do with it. But she did have feelings for Perry. Maybe it was all coincidence? Maybe he was being framed by them somehow? Why? For what reason?

She finally dialed.

"Jefferson County Sheriff's office. Detective Sergeant's desk."

"Look," the small voice came from the other end. " I didn't do anything."

"Hello?" the DS repeated. "I'm sorry. I didn't catch your name. Let's just start there."

She hesitated.

"Hello," he tried again. "Can we just start with a name?"

More silence as she pulled the phone away.

"Look, I can't help" he coaxed. "And I really want to. I can't help unless… "

"Candice… *Dee*… Dee Price."

"Miss Price," he leaned forward. "We've had difficulty locating you this evening. Is everything alright?"

"Like I said. I didn't do anything. And I don't know much, either. But last Sunday night Perry told me he might get a chance to do something for *The Family*."

"I'm sorry… *the family*?"

"Yeah, that's what they call themselves. Anyways, I'm leaving. Now. I'm so scared. The roads are bad. I don't care anymore."

"Miss Price. Dee. We can help. Just let us help. Have you been threatened in any way? By whom?"

"No, but I am not staying here another hour of my life to find out."

"Please… miss… "

Silence. Then the sound of a car shifting from park into drive.

"Omaha. That's all I know. Perry was starting in Idledale and headed to Omaha."

FRIDAY

THIRTY FOUR

Near Ogallah- Kansas

The farmer heard commotion, howling, and shuffling throughout the night.

Now it was near dawn and he had a shotgun in his heavily gloved hands. His boots crunched through each step, barely breaking its icy topmost inch. Now and then he'd find a softer patch and fall through to his knees. He'd just ascended from one when he stopped. He cleared his glasses and shined his flashlight forward.

"Good Lord," he mouthed against heavy winds.

FRIDAY- 4AM MST
Denver Field Office, FBI

She'd said to call at all hours. The DS just didn't expect *her* to be up at this hour. More likely some junior fed who majored in coffee and smoothie runs. The office sounded about right in the background for the hour of day. A few conversations, some keyboard clacking. Not much else.

"Agent Dickerson. Denver Bureau."

She warmed to the greeting on the other end.

"Detective Sergeant. Either you're calling in a breakfast burrito to the wrong number... or you have some info for me."

"Ha. Morning, agent. That does sound good right about now."

He got right to it, relating the call from Dee Price--Perry's girlfriend--and bringing Dickerson up to date on the findings at Townsend's place, which had amounted to exactly nothing to this point.

"I wish we had more."

"Please, sergeant," she circled Omaha on a digital map. "That's a huge break."

"Would be better if we had more. The girlfriend mentioned a family. No, *The Family*, like a proper name for the group of people in his life the last three years. She didn't like them, either."

"For good reason, sergeant."

"Agent?"

"Yeah."

"Anything else would be good to know on our end? What are we looking at here. Some kind of homegrown terror cell? White nationalists? I mean, that's been a major new focus for you guys, right?"

She weighed her words carefully. "Well, yes, and no. Are there small, disconnected groups of people very unhappy about the present and potential future of their country? Unhappy enough to want to do something about it? Sure, there's enough of those around to create headlines. And frankly, to make speeches in congress and from the White House sell better. So, from my vantage point, am I going to say no to increased funding? Not likely. And even though you won't hear it from those sources, there is a major distinction between a supremacist group and a separatist one of the same stripe. Not that they're unrelated, at least by basic beliefs. One wants to pretty much be left alone. Granted, being left alone requires significant control over their communities and if the entire country was run locally by separatists you'd have defacto national control. On the other hand, true supremacists, which we just haven't seen at scale for sixty-some years, really do want national control of culture, law, commerce. They still may imagine themselves as benevolent but they are definitely working from a framework of the "other being lesser," not just *other*.

But the number of these kinds of groups for whom we have actionable intelligence, even the beginnings of a file? Miniscule. Across the entire spectrum of potential threats we are watching this doesn't even land near the top by numbers. But your group? This *Family*? They seem to be moving the needle. Until now we'd been watching them as a separatist concern. Either they've significantly reworked their mission… "

"Likely?" the DS asked.

"No. Not at all, actually. Core beliefs rarely shift this way. I'd say they are looking to make a statement for others like them to follow. Or maybe they're just wanting to halt the advance of what they see as the opposing narrative. But now, thanks to your team we have a likely location of some kind of real-life op. We also now have a better sense of timing."

The DS wasn't following that last piece.

"Western Kansas. Only thirty minutes ago. Body found on a farm outside Ogallah."

"Never heard of it. And you guys must have really widened the net if you're catching any and all crime alerts across Kansas. "

"Yeah, like I said on our brief call yesterday, entire Greater Plains. Anyways, wolves making a huge fuss all night long. Guy gets up early and finds a car in one of his ditches at the edge of the field. Scratches all over the car from their claws but couldn't get in. Good thing, they would have torn him up real bad. So, no evidence yet but if we add the data point for the sake of conversation and then plot it out," she looked at her notes. "We have a likely route across Kansas and then up maybe at Topeka, or thereabouts. Let's just say he was making as good time as possible, having left Idledale early Wed AM. Give him an hour or so for the mishap, ah, alleged mishap in Ogallah."

"Midnight Wednesday or shortly thereafter. *No*," the DS let out.

"Agreed, sergeant. Perry Townsend is already there. And I'm sending you something. Did some digging after we talked yesterday. There," she clicked.

He saw the link and pulled it up.

CHI Health Arena Upcoming Events.

Friday, 7pm. Justice Now: A Call to Racial Reconciliation.

It was 6:30am in Western Iowa.

Carter was already up when he got the District 3 recall text. He kissed Mae as she was getting ready, grabbed his stuff and headed out the door. She wasn't happy he was going in on a scheduled day off but if they were recalling everyone, she could understand. And she could pray. Jons pulled into the parking lot, entered the building, and then grabbed a cup of the putrid substance posing as coffee before taking a seat in the conference room.

"HomeSec alert level was raised again as of ninety minutes ago," the shift sergeant began.

A few groans.

"Yeah, I get it," he continued. "This is for real. Intelligence leading to a major event in the Omaha - Council Bluffs area. Likely next twenty-four hours at 90%."

That got their attention. No alert in their area of operations had ever been authorized at anything near that certainty. Either the government had finally lost their minds, or they had something this time. Something very real and very dangerous.

"Likely next fourteen hours is… 85%."

That projection landed even heavier.

"Sarge?"

"Yep. I get it. Just means we need to get on this and now." He plugged his laptop into their smallish screen on the wall and continued. "Downtown Omaha. No games tonight. Creighton is away at Drake. Three probables, all being handled by Nebraska local and state cops, as well as FBI, HomeSec itself, and ATF. Henry Doorley… "

"The zoo, sarge?"

"Absolutely. Indoor capacity is decent. They've got a private group of about a thousand there over the weekend."

"Doing what?" another trooper asked.

The sergeant frowned. "Zoo stuff. That good enough for you?"

No reply.

"There's also a weekend series of seminars at Creighton, on campus, various buildings. All told about another thousand. Last… " They caught the sergeant's shift in tone. "CHI Health Arena. Tonight and into tomorrow. Social issues gathering, racial and justice system reform."

They waited.

"Ten thousand."

Everyone took a breath.

"Your assignments are in your folders. We have a couple of smaller gatherings on our side of the river. Casino ballroom sized, more like a few hundred. So, let's just be safe and assume maybe the intelligence was more like 'Omaha and surrounding areas.' If you're assigned to one of those sites, you'll be working alongside sheriff, city police, and Iowa-based feds. But mostly, if something bad happens today, you're either the help…" he paused. "Or the hammer. These roads are ours, troopers. No one causing harm, or even wanting to, is getting past us on the way out of Omaha. No one."

THIRTY FIVE

Omaha

The two white vans queued at security, just outside the service entrances to CHI Health Center Arena.

Richards was waved through first. He kept straight, with the wheel and his eyes. Townsend's fate was his own.

The guard looked over his paperwork. The upgrades had been scheduled for the last month. Nothing sudden. Multiple approvals. Then he looked over his features. Bushy hair. Glasses. A mustache just barely covered his upper lip. Perry sported none of these only a few hours ago. Richards supplied and applied them. He'd told Townsend you just couldn't be too careful. In reality, he knew who they'd be looking for, if it came to that, and he didn't want the younger man found out before they could complete the install. All available security bulletins showed no concern whatsoever regarding the two techs from *MidTown Digital*.

One more look and Townsend came through, as well.

They drove into the ready area and then under the actual structure. A short ramp led them downward where they found a spot to park. A large, blue "101" across the massive cement columns oriented them. They parked, got out, and got to work.

The two men removed eighteen-foot industrial ladders from each van, nicely racked on the passenger side exterior. They set them in place, approximately another eighteen feet apart. Richards opened his van and pulled out the first wiretrack section. He stepped up to where he could touch the existing cable runs beneath this section's interior seating. The bundles were already about six inches in diameter. Theirs would fit nicely, pulled up and above those already in place. Almost touching the steel understructure.

Richards pulled an o-ring clamp from his waist pouch. He nestled the terminated end of the first section up and in, sliding it through the clamp, tightening and then releasing. Townsend was standing about four feet away, holding the remaining sixteen feet of the run. Satisfied, Richards descended the ladder, moved it to where Perry was standing, and then repeated the process. With Richards halfway down the line Townsend placed his ladder back at the first clamp, tightening and double-checking the work. Five such dances later and the first twenty feet of their device was in place.

The work went fast. All the harder labor had been done the night before. Aside from the tracks feeling a little heavy--if you were for some reason to pick one up—it all looked so normal. Two guys doing their work to make a place like CHI Health do its job. You could almost imagine Mike Rowe showing up with a camera crew to wax folksy about the legions of laborers, making this fine country run.

Section 101. Then 102. 103.

At section 108 they were ordered to stop.

Swarms of law enforcement units moved throughout the arena and convention center.

The conference organizers, along with CHI Health staff, were being pulled aside and told to stay out of the way. They'd received no warning of the search.

How many were on site currently?

Not many, those in charge assured. Maybe a hundred among employees, pre-conference, and then the volunteers. But even most of them were not scheduled to arrive yet. Vendors would be here in a few hours.

We're going to need you to move off arena grounds. Please, be orderly and quiet about it.

"Move," Richards urged as more people came their way.

Townsend hesitated.

This time he pulled him roughly, over toward a temporary wall and then through to the other side. Piles of sheet rock and a few maintenance items lay strewn about.

"What's going on?"

"You," Richards accused. "You are what is going on."

Townsend blanched.

"Did you see their screens?"

No reply.

"Their screens, you idiot. iPads and phones. *Your* face on their screens. What did you… " he feigned, knowing full well the answer while revising his plans, even as he strung the younger man along.

"I… I don't… "

"Shut up!" he muffled. "I don't want to know. You just need to disappear for a while."

"But what if they… "

"They won't. And we're not done yet. We haven't even reached the 80% mark on the first side of the stadium."

"I don't know, man. We should just run. Yeah, run," he turned, only to be met with Richards' fist. He dropped hard and his eyes fell back into his head. The older man dragged him through three successive doors. Townsend snapped awake, putting his hands up to defend against another blow.

"Look," Richards grunted. "You need to get your act together. You can't run. At least not right now. And yes, that stupid disguise got you through the front door but that guard was an idiot. These are cops, trained to look past this kind of stuff. But if we hold tight, they'll leave. They're not going to find what, or who they're looking for."

"But," Perry was thinking a little more clearly now. "The conference. They'll cancel. No one here, even if we do finish our work."

"Listen," Richards let his sidearm show from inside his overalls. "I get paid for a destroyed building, one way or another. We are *finishing* our work before we leave. Now, put that bad hair and mustache back in place. Or do I have to do everything for you? Stay here. Stay quiet. I'll come get you. But it's going to be a while."

Richards moved quickly.

He returned to the place they left off their work.

Two Omaha Police Officers approached.

"Hey, need to see your ID and work orders. What you doin? Electronics?"

"Yeah, network and video upgrades. Here's the paperwork," he handed it over, trying his best to look innocently nervous.

The other officer looked toward the vans. "You got a partner here? Where is he?"

"Was in the head when you guys all came busting in. It's a little walk and he wasn't feeling so great earlier. Should be back in a bit. Should we be concerned? Is everything okay…"

The first officer grabbed his radio. "Henderson?"

"Henderson here."

"You at the security gate north side?"

"Yeah, here. What's up?"

"I got two techs here in the underbelly of the arena. Papers look good. Guard there seen the pics? He good with the visual of these guys from… ah, MidTown Digital?"

Henderson asked the question of the guard.

"Yep. Negative," he shot back. "Says neither of them match the suspect."

The guard even re-ran the video of their approach.

"Alright, then," the officer looked at Richards. "You and your partner need to clear out, off premises until we're done. We'll send him out when he comes back from the bathroom. Leave the vans and your tools. Go."

Richards walked away and then over to the area they wanted everyone to gather. He put on his best concerned look, even as he watched his time budget shrink.

Over the next two hours Richards sat with the others.

The Omaha officers got reassigned to another section of the building, releasing concerns they carried about a tech in the bathroom who had been cleared by security anyways.

Richards observed as teams looked, watched, talked, and tested. His van, as well as Townsend's had been the subject of intense, repeated scrutiny. Chem strips, radiation sticks. People and dogs. A knowledgeable ATF technician explained the new uses of bio-insulations in electronics applications to the others. He was impressed, hadn't known anyone in the Omaha area doing this kind of work.

Calmly, Richards watched them, agency by agency, signing off and walking away.

THIRTY SIX

"And that's exactly why the conference must go on."

The Agent In Charge was dumbfounded.

He had done his best to dissuade the senator's chief of staff.

"Of course," the chief replied. "She understands the risks. And she trusts the fine work you all have done this morning. The other sites? Anything there?"

"Initial reports back are all clean. But you can't be serious about this."

"You've accounted for all potential threats, have you not?"

"Yes, but the intel is very good. Chatter has only increased. This is far too high a profile event… and far too many potential casualties. Give me another twenty-four hours. Can we move it to Saturday?"

"Absolutely not. Just think of all the attendees. Why a gathering like this with ten thousand coming? That's travel from every state, and likely other parts of the world." Conveniently, the COS did not mention the senator's junket to the Bahamas beginning tomorrow. A private jet, courtesy of her big-pharma host, was going wheels up precisely at 8:00am. "And you know the optics," he continued. "We simply cannot allow the appearance of a win for these… these monsters. We hold the moral high ground. Our actions must show this at every turn."

"I have to say, respectfully, I think you're being foolish."

"Agent, I do appreciate your professionalism and frankness. But it's been decided. The organizers are on board, as well. CHI Health officials gave the green light. Why are we hesitating?"

These two assertions were also partially true. The senator disassociating from their organization was enough encouragement, with full assurances of safety, of course, to move them to keep the schedule. And the arena team had been presented with a development package estimated at twenty-three million dollars, stuffed deep within the new reparations bill. Willing news organizations had been briefed only that there were "enhanced security" measures being conducted at the arena. And then a single leak to a prominent social media influencer gave the scoop as to why. The senator's appearance was no longer a secret. They would use this for their own buzz, a marketing advantage. Ten hours stood between them and adoring crowds. That played perfectly for a last minute blitz. They might even sell out at the door.

"I don't know."

"I'm sorry. You don't know what?"

"Maybe this needs to go up the chain."

"Oh, agent," the COS marveled at his innocence. "It already has."

The troopers returned to District after wrapping up their assignments.

The Iowa side of the threat radius took until mid-morning to clear. Slowly, those not on actual patrol shifts came in from the cold and took their seats. The shift sergeant walked among the cobble of desks.

"If you're not driving, you're typing," he barked. "Feds want all reports into the database by noon."

Groans.

"*Noon*, ladies."

Bradford looked up.

"Yes. You, too."

Carter had been tasked to one of the larger tribal casinos in Council Bluff. Their head of security wasn't an easy introduction. Completely understandable. What better way to intrude where you normally had no jurisdiction. Emergency. Threat. Carter watched him weigh the intel and the risks against handing over his grounds and customers for a few hours. Who knew what they might find. Or, if you were the cynical type: manufacture. The security head was former Army and had been a very good hire. In a scenario with a high potential for misdeeds, he'd brought clear thinking along with honor, and the willingness to act. He'd also been bribed, and when that didn't work, threatened. Sometimes by the very people with a badge and an oath.

Carter tred lightly. "Sir, would it be possible to take a look at your camera feeds?"

He'd looked Jons over for a few seconds. New to the job. He had all the earmarks of a young trooper. Too early in his career to be a problem. But there was more than that. Something about him said *proceed*.

Carter stepped into the cramped room. A desktop workspace extended everywhere a door wasn't. Above the counters hung more monitors than he'd ever seen in one place, except maybe the tv section of a Best Buy. One particular set of tri-monitors caught his attention. The imagery held a wireframe outline of a human skull.

"Recognition software?" Carter marveled.

"Yep. Quite fast, really good."

Carter pulled his phone out and swiped. Perry Townsend's alert picture was at the ready.

"Done."

"I'm sorry. What?" Carter replied.

"We monitor Homeland Security here, as well, Trooper Jons. Mr. Townsend came back as negative for the last forty-eight hours on premises. And we're running a new scan every hour. My entry teams are also using their portable units."

"Portable?"

"Yes. A little slower than the hardware in this room. Still, quite powerful and useful. I can guarantee you this man has not entered our buildings."

Satisfied, Carter headed back downstairs. He walked the floor calmly. Hardly anyone looked up. They had not busted in and demanded everyone be evacuated for a search and questioning. The law was not in their favor for such an entrance, anyways. Now, after checking in with their team it became clear this was not a place under immediate threat, at least from Perry Townsend. The MO also made little sense. True, it was of a reasonable capacity to fall within the minimum datapoints for investigation. And yes, there could be some measure of racial components to an attack at a place such as this.

The trooper thought back to the briefing.

Perry Townsend. Thirty-two. Caucasian male. Small town west of Denver. Associations with a group harboring some level of white separatist leanings. Above ground media — social and web — was generically far-right, distrust of government kind of stuff. A smattering of prepper with a few good conspiracies thrown in. Over the last three years they'd been all talk, not even a hint of action. No connection with gatherings, protests. The last six months, though, their dark web presence had kicked it up a notch.

Communication, research. All began pointing to the potential of harm. But this kind of ideology had a normal range of targets. Native American Tribes were not high on that list.

Carter finished up his report and pushed "send."

"Sarge," he leaned over. "Alert suspended?"

"Ah, yeah, Jons. Officially, as of … ten minutes ago. If you're done, you can head out."

"Might as well stay through lunch. I got a couple other items sitting on my list. Couple of emails. You know, non-terrorist kind of stuff."

"Got it. Well," the sergeant paused. "Good work out there. Would love to get a hold of that piece of… " he remembered Carter used to be a pastor. "But… yeah, glad it's nothing. At least for now. But this guy's gonna make a mistake. Bet on it."

Carter doubted he intended the pun but received the props anyways. "Thanks, sir."

Jons leaned forward, toward his screen. He scanned the files from the alert again. Something didn't feel right. It stayed with him as walked into the next room, opened the fridge and eyed Mae's enchiladas through a clear plastic container.

"Thirty seconds oughta do it."

He sat down. For the first time in a long time he stopped to bow his head, thanking the Lord for the leftovers currently warming in the break room microwave. He also spent a few extra seconds asking for insight, guidance. If there was something they weren't seeing, he wanted to be open to leading from the Spirit.

THIRTY SEVEN

They finally received the okay to continue.

Law enforcement had checked off. Same with the CHI Health staff. The installation was a needed upgrade and they wanted it ready for the conference open if at all possible.

Would there still be time?

Oh, that's wonderful.

And, I have to say, our first contract with you will definitely lead to more in the near future.

Richards grabbed his ladder and put it into place at Section 108.

Townsend walked around the corner. His version of nonchalant needed some work.

"You look guilty," Richards murmured while hauling another twenty-foot section from his van. "Get over here. Keep your head low and we'll get this done."

"You sure?"

"Gonna have to step it up. Down to fifteen minutes a section. Don't worry so much about the tighten and check. Not like the install needs to last long term, anyways."

It sounded especially cold.

"So," Perry kept his voice down. "Conference looks like it's still on. That's crazy."

"Not at all, kid. See, you just need a little faith. I thought you'd be all about that kind of thing."

The men moved even more efficiently than before. Section 108. 109. 110. Half of their device was in place. Packing up their tools and re-attaching the ladders they drove another few hundred feet, around the arena's curve. At Section 116 they resumed.

Clamps went up. Track hung. Connectors seated. 117. 118. 119. At Section 120 a clamp broke. It took another minute from their revised budget to replace it.

Vendors were now swarming the place. Foodservice trucks came in the same entrance they'd used. Richards and Townsend had cleared the initial security checks as well as a major law enforcement search. Being discovered? That wasn't so much the concern. More people meant they would have to accommodate others' needs for the already slim working spaces they were utilizing. That was definitely not a part of the original plan. Musicians came in and needed an extra wide berth for their gear to get through to the staging area. That slowed them down for a good half-hour. The additional lighting crew got their lifts stuck right where MidTown Digital was working at Section 122. Another forty-five minutes there. Lastly, the under areas of the arena were not well heated. The duo's hands were getting colder by the minute. It was harder to fasten, harder to tighten. A few times screwdrivers dropped when both were on a ladder. None of these were game changers, but all told they were adding up.

"I dunno."

Richards gave Townsend another look. Then he caught the time on his phone. "We're good. Just stay on it. We'll be fine."

This time the man was not in his expansive living room overlooking the mountains.

He was at the mill, in his smallish but reasonably appointed office. Of the other two usually present for these conversations, only one was here now.

"So?"

"All is well," the mill owner replied.

"How *exactly* do you know?"

"Calm down, things are moving forward."

"Again, I need to ask... how do you know? Did you break communication silence over normal channels?"

A pause.

"What!? Please, tell me you weren't... "

"Weren't... *what*?"

No answer.

"No," he continued. "I was not stupid. And we needed slightly more details passed than what was possible over the dark web app. The emails passed through seven different filtered sites. Each one had an address redirect. Literally all over the world. Likely the NSA has tagged them? Maybe. But will they untangle them... ever? No, they will not. That was a one-time usage and the accounts have been completely eliminated. No traces. Come," he motioned. "You need to calm yourself. We are so close, now. So very close."

"But, I thought our *employee* would only use the dark web methods."

"My communications were not with our employee."

The revelation shocked the other man. He would have been even more surprised to know the details.

"The senator's people are good to go, what's the problem?"

The small room on the second floor of CHI Health arena had become a very tense place in the last few minutes of the morning's search. The conference team was split over calling it all off or going ahead.

"Terri," Dennis caught what had happened. "Wait, you've confirmed with the senator's people? Why? That's not your place at all on this committee. We asked you to interface with them, but that decision was not yours to make."

"Well, someone needed to get it done."

"Wait just a minute! You haven't even been with us the whole time. What, you joined up six months ago? And now you just think you can unilaterally move decisions forward that have this much at stake?"

"CHI Health is fine with it, too. And there's not exactly a terror-threat-resolved clause for us financially."

The budget. This had been so far removed from any other event they'd ever put on. The scale here was something very different. Even with two major donors it was still barely possible. They'd been able to sell enough tickets, yes. But was money really a good enough reason to put this many people in harm's way? Even if all had been cleared, wasn't there still a threat out there somewhere?

"She'll pull us from the list."

"You can't be serious."

"That's something they wanted me to communicate, very clearly. We'll fold. Research. Grants. Events. Progress. Done. There's a hundred other groups like us out there. She doesn't need us. We most definitely need her. Now… we still have a mountain of things to do before doors open in a little over eight hours."

A pause. And then reluctant nods across the room.

The door opened.

"Where are you going? You just said we had a mountain of things to do."

"One of those things, Dennis. I left my laptop across the hall. Just need to send an email."

"There's someone else?"

The man steamed even more as he paced around the mill office. "Have you gone completely insane!?"

Richards and Townsend placed the final run of track at Section 126.

The men pulled their ladders down and headed over to Richards' van. He pulled out his phone. An app came up with the seating map of CHI Health on it. He tapped a few tiles and the sections all turned green. He smiled. Two more conductivity checks and he'd be assured they were ready. He tapped the same tiles. Again, all green. He waited thirty seconds and then tapped them again. This time he got a blinking orange across the majority of the second half of the install, Sections 116-123.

124-125 were grayed out.

Townsend saw it and moved quickly toward the van door.

The door locks clicked before he could get to the handle.

"We're not going anywhere until we fix this."

THIRTY EIGHT

Justyn's breathing had slowed but his wheezing had not.

Every breath was labored. He was bringing up blood with every cough. The young man had been mostly unconscious through the night and early morning. The single bar of reception on his phone had appeared as a blessing. But the single bar just wasn't enough to connect. He'd tried. Twenty-seven times before giving up. Now he just wondered if it was some form of divine joke. Maybe this was a form of the judgment coming his way. Or maybe he still hadn't relented. What was that story? He strained to pull it out of his now-addled memory. Everything was slow, so foggy.

God wants a man to do something. The man says no and runs away. A ship? Yes, he gets onto a ship. Storms, everywhere. Waves pulling the vessel apart at the seams. People are scared. They're all going to die very soon. A horrible death at sea. He realizes it's his fault, the others are innocent. The man jumps into the ocean. He wakes up in the belly of a fish. Such a weird story.

Carter felt a tug in his spirit.

He resisted.

That's not how it works. I'm a seminary-trained pastor. You don't just hear a text reference and open it up. You study and then apply…

He felt it again.

"Okay," he prayed at his desk. "But this is super weird." He opened his Bible, right there.

Now the LORD provided a huge fish to swallow Jonah, and Jonah was in the belly of the fish three days and three nights. From inside the fish Jonah prayed to the LORD his God.

He said: In my distress I called to the LORD, and he answered me. From deep in the realm of the dead I called for help, and you listened to my cry. You hurled me into the depths, into the very heart of the seas, and the currents swirled about me; all your waves and breakers swept over me.

I said, 'I have been banished from your sight; yet I will look again toward your holy temple.' The engulfing waters threatened me, the deep surrounded me; seaweed was wrapped around my head. To the roots of the mountains I sank down; the earth beneath barred me in forever. But you, LORD my God, brought my life up from the pit.

When my life was ebbing away, I remembered you, LORD, and my prayer rose to you, to your holy temple. Those who cling to worthless idols turn away from God's love for them. But I, with shouts of grateful praise, will sacrifice to you. What I have vowed I will make good. I will say, "Salvation comes from the LORD."

And the LORD commanded the fish, and it vomited Jonah onto dry land.

Jonah 1:17 - 2:10

"Okay, Lord," Carter asked. "What am I supposed to do with that?"

The phone went to two bars.

Justyn squinted. His head dangled. He was so tired. Still, he tried one more time.

Dialing…

"911. Is this an emergency?"

Nothing in reply.

"911. If this is not an emergency, please hang up and call your local police or fire services."

"Unghhhh,"

"Hello?"

"Hellllp… "

Click.

"In my distress I called to the Lord and He answered me."

Carter looked around the room.

"Okay. Yeah. Jonah had to get to his lowest point before he was willing to surrender. In his case it was actually death. Lord, are you trying to tell me something about myself, or someone else?"

He couldn't shake the sense this was a holy moment. In all honesty, he didn't want to. He hadn't felt this connected in, well, it had been a long time. But he could at least continue the conversation somewhere else. He grabbed his Bible and headed to the gym. He was officially off the clock, so no problem there. With his elbows on his knees he looked down at his Bible on the wooden floor.

The currents swirled about me; all your waves and breakers swept over me.

"Your waves. Your breakers. I have to say, Lord, that doesn't feel right at times. It's really hard to hang onto Your goodness when things are crashing and they're in Your world, Your control."

"911. Is this… "

"Pleeeease," Justyn cried. Then he coughed up more red.

"Sir, are you hurt? Can you give me your location?"

"Van…. Snow."

"Have you been in an accident? Are there others?"

"No one… else."

"Can you give me anything, landmarks, roads?"

"Trees… farm road," he was failing, thoughts and words requiring far more than he had in him.

Silence.

"Sir? Sir… "

Click.

Justyn rotated, painfully, only to see the signal had dropped again.

Carter's heart sped.

"I know. I know I've got a lot of growing to do. Thank you for bringing me to my end. Mercifully, God."

To the roots of the mountains I sank down; the earth beneath barred me in forever. But you, LORD my God, brought my life up from the pit.

"I... I can't."

"Sir," the voice pleaded. "You sound like you're in a lot of pain. I really want to help you. Do you have your location finder on?"

Justyn had been instructed to turn it off. He knew he'd not be able to flip through the settings anyways. It was taking everything he had for a simple call.

"Wait," he pleaded. "Please… please don't go."

"I'm not going anywhere, sir. I promise."

"Dying," he coughed.

"Lord, I can't help but think this is for somebody else, too."

There were no words, no voice. Just a keen clarity that this ancient text had a dual purpose for Carter on this particular day.

"But, who? C'mon. You gotta help me out here. I want to be Your vessel, Lord. Do your work. You put me here and now I really, really think You're speaking to me. Please, God. Show me what's next. Show me."

What I have vowed I will make good. I will say, "Salvation comes from the LORD."

The signal faded as more foul weather passed through.

"Sir... you're breaking up quite a bit now. Can you move at all? Find a better spot for reception?"

"Doesn... tter...too... ate... "

"Sir... "

"...maha... "

The line clicked off again. The silence brought tears of desperation. He'd had no hope for so long. A person on the other end was now surprisingly important to him. He felt himself slipping further away. Everything was shutting down. His vision began fading, even as his eyes seemed to not blink, at least not very often.

The story came back. The man in the fish cried out for help.

Justyn forced his eyes shut and remembered his first words after the crash and coming to. He still wasn't ready. Now, only one word was all he could get out. Three letters, from the very bottom of his soul.

"God... "

THIRTY NINE

"Jons?"

Carter's head snapped up at the shift sergeant's voice.

"Buckner. Buckner Feed & Seed. Got a hit."

"Sarge?"

"I mean, unless you're not interested anymore."

Carter grabbed his Bible, thinking this could be his answer. Or maybe just more good policing to be done. "Absolutely, sir. Who? Where?"

"McClelland. Quick Stop owners there. Donald," he read his notes "... and Judy. Baxter. Husband says he got a quick image of the van running past his store early afternoon Tuesday."

"He waited until now?"

"Just saw the CAB from Wednesday. Sat in his email. Super apologetic. Says his inbox had recently been 'organized' and now he can't find anything. But he was very clear about the vehicle and the sign. I know you're not on, Jons, but thought I'd give you first shot since it seemed to sit in your craw a bit more than others."

Honestly, Carter had mostly forgotten about it since the tow theory failed and his interaction with...

"Bradford!" the shift sergeant yelled into the hallway.

"Sarge?" she answered, stepping into the gym. "Jons. I hope you're working on your drop step in here, 'cause to be straight up, it sucks."

Carter pretty much agreed on that one.

She noticed the Bible. "And I don't think even The Almighty can help you with that dumpster fire of a mid range jumper."

"Look," the sergeant continued. "The van with changed plates…"

"No," she interrupted. "Please, sarge. I've done enough of this guy's work already. And didn't we lay that one to rest?"

"New tip," Carter offered.

"Better be good if we're heading out in this slop."

"I guess we'll see," the sergeant explained. "And that's exactly why I'm sending the both of you."

A new weather cell had arrived over the southwestern edge of the state and it was coming on hard.

Carter and Bradford were heading through it as they dove east on State Route 6. What should have taken twelve minutes expanded into twenty-five. Even then, they had to take a graveled road north to reconnect to G61. Three cars had spun out a mile further. Local police had it handled but the troopers still needed to backtrack slightly before advancing toward McClelland.

Thirty-Seven minutes later they pulled up outside the Quick Stop. They shut down their cruisers and headed inside. The bell rang as Carter knocked dirty ice and snow against the store's threshhold.

"Ma'am," Carter started. "Trooper Jons. Trooper Bradford is on her way in. Got your tip about the van just a bit ago and headed on over. You open all day today?" he looked back through the sweaty glass. "Bad out there."

"Yep," Judy agreed. "Hasn't been this bad in a while. Maybe four years ago. February. But it's bad today, for sure."

Bradford stepped in. "Ma'am."

"Hello, trooper," she greeted. "Can I get either of you something hot to drink? Maybe something sweet? Baked goods? Mid-day but still tasty."

"Oh, no. But thanks," Bradford answered. "We won't take much of your time. A couple questions, that's all."

"Oh, alright. But I am not sending you back out there without something."

Both troopers sized her up, knowing an argument would be fruitless, and just smiled.

"Certainly," Carter relented.

"Don?" she sent her voice down the slim hallway at back. "Don, state troopers here."

"Oh, oh," her husband's voice floated back. He was out after some shuffling, the same welcoming presence as Judy.

"Mr. Baxter," Bradford started. "Thank you so much for a little bit of time this afternoon."

"Not at all, trooper. I am so sorry I didn't see it earlier. Hope it wasn't as important as it sounds it may have been. Community Awareness Bulletins. I always try to look for those. But... well, something changed in my email and now I can't find a dang thing anywhere."

"We'd heard. That happens to me all the time," she assured.

Carter noted the softness.

"Well. Me and the missus, we run a pretty small ship here. But we got these cameras and such. Have to go through them every day."

"Are you using videotape?" Bradford continued.

"Oh, heavens no," Don laughed. "We're way more up to date than that. Computer. Hard drive. But we don't like to pay for those monthly storage fees on the web."

"Cloud," Judy interjected.

"Huh?"

"Cloud. It's stored on some 'cloud.' Were you listening at all?"

"Cloud. Web. Whatever," Don shot back. "Not paying for it wherever it goes."

Carter kept his laugh under wraps. This was totally going to be he and Mae down the road at some point.

"Like I was saying," Don reset. "Computer hard drive. Gets full. So we have to keep up on things. Wednesday," he thought back. "Yep, Wednesday. Reviewing the files from day before. Nothing. Nothing. And a whole lot more nothing. Then he just speeds right by."

"The van," Carter stepped in. "Buckner Feed & Seed?"

"Exactly. Which I thought was weird. So I wrote it down."

"Weird?"

"Yep, for two reasons. One, no need for another Feed & Seed in McClelland. Ol' Jim's been open for thirty years. Doing the town just fine."

"Got it. And reason number two?"

"He was going too fast. Blizzard out there on Tuesday afternoon. Just buzzed right by. I slowed down the video to check. Be surprised if he could see anything more than a few feet. Way too fast."

"Ok," Bradford stepped back in. "So the video file?" she hoped for a different answer than presumed.

"Sorry, again. Deleted. Gotta keep the hard drive space. I hope this is still helpful for you two."

Judy set them up before they walked out. "I really hope you find what you're looking for. And it's so nice to see partners working so well, together. You know, that really is me and Don's secret."

"Oh," Bradford replied. "We're not… "

The troopers left with more thanks, as well as a bag and a cup for each.

Sitting in their respective cruisers, they eyed the sweetrolls.

Carter dialed Bradford's cell. She hit "answer" as the car idled. Jons' voice came over bluetooth.

"Thoughts?"

"Almost as good as my great aunt's. Almost."

"Huh? Oh, yeah. Haven't tried mine yet. How about the van."

"Not much there, Jons. Unless you're seeing something I'm not, which we both know… "

"Yeah, I get it. No. I mean, probably not."

"Jons. You're thinking something. I can hear the wheels creaking from over here," she waved.

"Ah, Okay. Well, so Tuesday I was on this very same road, afternoon patrol. I think our van may have been the guy that almost ran me off the road in that whiteout."

"That would be quite the coincidence. Odds on that? You're the numbers guy, right?"

"I know, I know. Astronomical. At least before the video placing him here same time as me. Nearly ended up in the ditch. Got out and inspected. Everything okay. But then while I was outside I heard… "

"Oh, yeah," she laughed. "Trees. Scared the daylights out of you."

"Not scared," Jons clarified. "I mean, yeah, I jumped. A little. But it was so loud. I'd never heard branches snap like that. Even under the duress of freezing ice."

"So, let me get this straight, Jons. You're thinking maybe that van never got out of McClelland?"

"I don't know. Maybe?"

"Alright. I'll bite. As long as I get to stay inside my car. Let's drive around."

FORTY

It was only getting worse.

"Slow is steady."

Bradford's quip usually applied to firing a weapon, especially under return fire. Made good sense now as they paced themselves down G61 with visibility at around twenty to thirty inches. Headlights played out quickly, creating a flash of luminance after that. Almost counterproductive.

"Southeast clear."

"Northwest good."

They'd decided to each focus on one side of the road, covering it with two sets of eyes instead of glancing back and forth.

5mph. They couldn't go any faster. Carter led. Bradford stayed in his rear lights.

"Old farm road is what we're looking for," she said. "Just keep us straight and it should be on my side. Southeast."

Carter was moving forward without any way of stopping quickly. All he had was the space in front of his car and then a glowing white wall. His wipers were keeping up fine. He just didn't have any sightline beyond the snow in front of him. His tires gripped okay. It was blowing so hard. Waves of powder went right to left, not able to drop onto the pavement and make a difference.

"Bradford."

"Yeah. See something?"

"No, not yet." He'd wanted to find a way to start the conversation he knew they had to have. Sometimes a common focus helps set up a hard talk. And did he really want to have this one face to face? Maybe the buffer of the cruisers was a good thing? Why not. "I just."

"You just what?"

"Look, Bradford. We've had a rough time finding our footing."

"You could say that. It's clear we don't see eye to eye on a few things."

"Sure, but it feels like more than that. Are we gonna butt heads forever? Stuff seems to escalate with us pretty fast."

"Well, Jons. Like I've said a few times. There's a lot you don't know."

"Like Pleasanton."

Her grip slipped for just a second.

Carter continued. "Sarge told me. Right after… "

"Oh yeah? He did? And what exactly did he tell you?" Carter heard the tension rising from the car in back.

"I read. And, I watched the documentary. Your grandad… "

She was silent.

"He," Carter added. "Amazing. I can see where you get it from."

"Yeah? So, you read. You watched a movie."

"Bradford. It made me sick."

"And now everything is just fine, right? All good. Mr. White Male Carter Jons feels bad, absolved henceforth of all connections and responsibilities."

"Hey, I just… "

"*Stop.*"

He did.

"We just passed it. Back up, turn left."

The snow on the old farm road had more chance to gather, slightly below grade of the main road.

The cruisers' tires sunk deeper, slid a bit with very few feet. Both troopers kept their vehicles on the road. After all, driving in adverse conditions had been one of their core focuses during the twenty-week DPS Academy, their basic training. Seventy more days of field exposure and they were sworn in, moving from peace officer candidate to Trooper 2's. Carter, six months post graduation, was so thankful for the training.

"Getting heavier," Carter offered.

"Woods bigger than usual here."

"Think they farmed them as well?"

"Could be. Most times they just needed a wind break for the homestead. So much open land all around. A few lines make a big difference. But these, these are huge. Much thicker. Looks like it could go back a mile from here. If they farmed these, at some point just got left to grow on their own. No thinning. No management."

"Bradford… "

"Not now, Jons."

His tacit agreement was communicated in silence, moving slowly forward along the road. They got to an old fenceline, clearly marked for no trespassing, even for hunters. The snow was much deeper beyond the gate.

"Turn around?" Bradford offered. "I didn't see anything."

"Me, neither. Okay. Let's head back."

What should have been an easy three-point turn became much harder. Carter and Bradford struggled equally. A few inches forward. Another few back. Even rocking their cruisers to get out of small crevices created by their tires. Finally, they were facing back down the old farm road and out to G61.

"District dispatch" the radio crackled. "This is 3. Bradford. Jons. Copy?"

He answered. As did she.

"Been a minute. You guys having too much fun out there to come back in? Snow angels. Igloos? Wait, with you guys it was a snowball fight, right? But more like iceballs."

"Dispatch, this a routine comm check? Or you got something we need to know," Bradford cut to the chase.

"Ah, yeah. 911 distress call. Well, actually multiples."

"Multiple distress calls?" Carter asked.

"Multiple calls, same number."

"And you're going to tell us why this matters to us, right now, out here?" Bradford pressed.

"Absolutely. Took a while because there was some kind of cloaking on the number. 911 operator had some connections and got it tagged. Probably has a cousin at some federal agency... "

"And... "

"Triangulated from three towers. Pinged it down to within a four hundred foot radius."

He paused. "Super weird, but... you're there."

"What?"

"Right in the center of it."

"You said I was going to get to stay in my car, Jons."

The troopers pulled their parkas tight and stepped out into the blinding white.

The temperature had actually risen over the last few days. Among Midwesterners' superpowers, they oddly enough know the real difference between zero degrees, or less, and simply sub-freezing. One will kill you. One you just need to be smart. And yes, anything above 30 is shorts weather. Earlier in the week it would have been much harder. This afternoon, at twenty degrees Fahrenheit, they'd have fifteen or so minutes of exposure before having to seek shelter. Their search lunges would have to be organized, precise. At least as best they could in the howling winds and continued snowfall.

Backup, as well as fire and rescue, were on the way, District had assured. But the troopers were there now and it would be at least thirty to forty five minutes. They could make two to three attempts on their own. Last known call was over an hour ago, so no guarantees, even if they should find whomever this was. And if this was their van after all, were they walking blindly into danger? More like stumbling. This was a rescue, for now. If it became an apprehension the conditions would seriously degrade their situational awareness, their ability to act and react. District said the caller was near-death. Well, that could mean weakness. It could also mean desperation.

"Stay within my beam," Bradford yelled above the winds. "Sweep left. Follow me."

Carter did as directed. Each step was a challenge. The ground just off the road became uneven. The snow was hard one second, powder the next. They were falling and getting back up as much they were walking. Trudging forward, they made their presence known as best they could.

"Iowa State Troopers!"

"Anyone?!"

"Can you hear us!?"

"Anyone?!"

FORTY ONE

The first two search runs led to nothing.

They'd made their way across a decent patch of the north side of the road. But every fifteen minutes only ended in frustration, coming back to their vehicles to regain some feeling in their faces and try to mark somehow in their minds where they'd just been. Flares helped. But those were few and far between.

Their gear was holding up okay. State-issue outerwear was pretty good. Still, Carter lost just a little bit of feeling in his left hand that last go around. He took an extra two minutes this time with his hands as close to the dash heat vents as possible.

Fifteen minutes later, they were back inside again.

"Jons," Bradford came across the phone line. "You holding up?"

"Yeah, doing okay."

"I just thought, you know, with your advanced age and all."

He appreciated the attempt.

"What do you think," she asked.

"I don't know. Seems like we've covered that north side pretty well, to me. Any further out and we're way into the woods. Chances of a distress call from there? I mean, exposure out here. There's no structures anywhere. Farm buildings fell to dust a long time ago. Or burned. Who knows?"

"Yeah, agreed. We go southside next."

They both paused.

"It looks frozen," Carter finally said.

"The creek."

"Yeah, I saw it, too. Forty feet off the road or so that direction. Didn't get a great look but seemed pretty thick."

"Let's hope so. We fall through and into water? Not good. Extra careful over there."

Both troopers were breathing a little heavy now. Their bodies were fighting the cold and the stress of the search. Still, they stepped out and onto the other side of the road.

"Hey," Bradford pointed.

Up the farm road. Barely. Lights and the muffled sounds of wheels on snow.

Four more trooper cruisers were making their way, red and blue flashing, headlights on full. Behind them came two snow removal units. Tracked and with large blades, they cleared a path for the fire and ambulance to proceed. It seemed like momentum.

"Can't believe it."

Carter agreed, though Bradford couldn't see his head nodding from inside his cruiser. They both held a high degree of hope that last run would be it.

"How many calls did dispatch say, again?"

"Three. Pretty quick succession. And they said the reception was terrible. Like to think we could just call the guy up but the triangulation was via sim card identifier, not phone number. 911 couldn't even see it on their end."

"Maybe the coordinates weren't right. Maybe they just made a math error."

"Jons. We're doing everything we can."

"Are we?" his frustration spilled over.

"Yeah, I get it. But yeah, we are. And so are they," she referenced the snowplows, working hard and the other troopers, now out and increasing the search radius. "If this guy was out in the open, he's dead. If he was in the van we're looking for, or any other kind of vehicle, where is he? I mean, sure, visibility is horrendous, but at some point you cover all the area, even if it's a few feet at a time. If he's hiding, it's in plain sight. Maybe, just maybe, if he calls again they can test the location again. Maybe refine it a little more for us."

"You get the transcripts yet?"

"Yeah, email just landed with attachment. You don't have them?"

Carter pulled his phone up. "Nope. Not yet. I'd like to take a look. Maybe there's something there that could be helpful. Airdrop them to me?"

She opened her phone settings, "saw" his phone within range, and sent the documents.

The thought hit both of them at the same time.

They spread out again.

This time they had their phone settings open, bluetooth on and scanning for any potential airdrop recipients. The restricted range of thirty feet was challenge enough. They'd also attached their gloves at their sides, wanting quick reaction on the screen but also knowing they'd need to put them back every few minutes. Their fingers got cold, very quickly. Two minutes off, two minutes on was the agreed rhythm.

"C'mon, c'mon" Carter urged, falling into some snow again. "Gotta be here. Gotta be here somewhere."

Four minutes. Six.

"Bradford?!"

"Here!" through the continued winter swirl.

"Anything?"

"No. Gotta head back to the cruiser for a few. Get back there, now, Jons."

He turned and saw her gloves at her side. And then her fingers.

"Bradford!"

And then the iPhone showed up.

"Can't," he breathed. "Get back into the car. Get those gloves on, now. We had an agreement. I'll pull my cruiser back, should be within range."

They both got back inside his car, it was closest. He put it into reverse and eased back to where they'd found the signal. Now it was gone from Carter's phone. Too far. He drove another five feet. Nothing. Seven more feet and he was as close to the edge of the road as he dared, the drop into the creekbed dangerously close now. Another three inches…

"Stop," Bradford ordered, for the second time this afternoon. *"There… "*

She handed the phone to Carter. "My fingertips are not working all that well at the moment."

Justyn could barely see.

But he could hear. With only 5% battery left his phone lit up and dinged.

Airdrop request: Carter Jon's iPhone.

It had to be an error. Some delayed system item. Or maybe his phone was doing weird things too, just like his mind.

Ding.

Airdrop request: Carter Jon's iPhone.

With great effort he tapped *accept.*

A text document landed.

He tapped that.

Received your 911 distress calls. On site and within 30 feet. Searched above ground. Will begin excavating snowbank. Hold on. Can you tap out a message and airdrop to us? If not, send back this document and we'll proceed with yes or no questions. Send back our documents once as a 'yes' and twice as a 'no.'

Justyn got another, and he guessed, his final, sense of reasonable lucidity. He'd pulled his glove off his right hand with his teeth to dial 911. Able to get it back on part way, his fingertips were still usable. But with that simple exertion everything hurt again and he realized how immobile he'd been since the calls. He'd simply been waiting to die.

Able to cradle the phone against a flat part of the van's destroyed interior, he held his pointer against his thumb to steady it and tapped the keyboard laboriously, and not that accurately.

Airdrop request: iPhone.

Carter's heart jumped.

"Yes!" Bradford said.

Accept.

Ding.

Carter was excited to see a new document come back. "Okay, maybe a little better than yes or no's."

He tapped the icon.

Carfl dig. Wat er. Hurre. Nme s Justn.

FORTY TWO

Five brave souls from the local fire station dug with everything they had.

I t was an almost entirely volunteer unit. They began at thirty-five feet out from the embankment. Spread out as evenly as they could, they kept pace with each other to make sure the snowbanks were being displaced proportionately. With the mix of ice and snow, the binding qualities were tricky to gauge and could come apart in huge chunks. Too much and all would be out of balance for their burgeoning crater. The last thing they wanted to do was partially uncover the victim—now known as Justn—only to trigger an avalanche.

Carter and Bradshaw had been ordered out of the way. They stayed in his cruiser, sending messages and impatiently awaiting the rapidly deteriorating replies.

"He's fading," Bradford noted.

"Yeah. Feels like he's losing his grip. I mean, on the long end he's been down there for almost three days at this point."

Three days.

Carter side-eyed Bradford.

"Would you mind if I pray?"

"Not my thing," she looked over. "But hey, no law against it. And trust me, I've studied it."

"I mean," he clarified. "Would you mind if I pray out loud, like here. I think we're running out of time. And I think this guy is who I heard… I mean, thought about when I was reading my Bible earlier."

"In the gym, *that's* what you were doing? And you thought about some guy buried in a field under who knows how much snow and ice?"

"No. More like I had a sense… that what I was reading was going to matter for me, and someone else today."

She shrugged.

"God," Carter prayed. "We need a for real miracle. I can't imagine you brought us here to let this man die. I don't know him, don't know who he is or what he's possibly done. But we'll never know if we can't get him out of there in time. Father, you made everything. You have all the power and control needed here. So many times in scripture You stepped in when our strength fails. I'm not even sure what I'm asking for. But, please move your hand and help us rescue this man."

Bradford opened her eyes awkwardly. "Well, sounds like you know the guy. Hope he likes you."

They both waited.

Nothing.

The firemen continued their labors.

The troopers hadn't received an airdropped message in nearly ten minutes.

She almost looked embarrassed for him.

He felt perhaps a little silly. Maybe presumptuous.

"Jons," she said. "Never hurts to ask… "

Overhead, a massive cracking sound rang out.

"Get back!" the fire captain yelled. "Back! Now!"

Everyone at the edges bailed, leaving their shovels where they lay.

Three pine limbs, all over fifteen feet long, began their violent release from a towering trunk. Each let go, seeming to launch away from their parent. The impact was enormous, right in the middle of their work area. Right on top of where they believed a man lay dying.

Everyone froze.

"Don't move!" the captain yelled. "This whole thing could go."

It started slowly. Then a huge middle section of snow began to shift, a giant glacier of icy topped powder. It likely weighed hundreds of pounds. Momentum carried it to the side and down, pulling evermore snow in its wake. Sheets grabbing, yanking. The veil of white was overwhelming. More ferocious than an ocean wave. More like a wintry earthquake and landslide all in one. An icy flow fell to the side and into the open space. It broke through, hit water at bottom, spraying back up to the top.

Bradshaw and Carter gaped from the cruiser. They both ran outside just in time to see the revealed undercarriage of a Ford Transit van. At least what remained. The forces weighed against this vehicle while underground had been enormous, played across every surface, every weld, every curve.

A now-exposed rear bumper held a mangled plate.

Iowa License: *HVH 129.*

Carter leaned cautiously forward, taking two more steps until he could see the graphic.

Buckner Feed & Seed.

The winds had died down, making communication easier.

Carter looked to the captain.

"Not sure, trooper. Wouldn't trust it just yet. Sure would be good to know what condition he's in. That shell of a vehicle is so compromised. One false move."

Considering the upheaval that had just taken place, all was eerily quiet. No pounding. No screaming. It spoke volumes.

"That had to be horrible from the inside." Carter reflected. "Even given what he's likely been through already. We've got to move now, captain."

"Hey," another fireman yelled. "Over here. This side. A branch"

It was the oddest thing they'd seen on what was a very strange afternoon. Six inches around. Piercing the van tomb and sticking straight up about twelve feet.

"How did we not see that?" Bradford marveled. "Was it always there, just beneath the snowpack? Good, Lord. Is that how he breathed?"

"Could be," Carter replied. "And if it's carrying air in and out, then… "

The captain eyed Carter, knowing what he was thinking. "No way. Let us handle it."

"Captain, we don't have time for this. I've been messaging him. He knows me, at least a little. The van's activity is suspicious. If there's anything to know… "

"About what?"

"That's the point, sir. We don't know. But I don't want to take a chance we miss something here. And," he paused. "If these are his last few moments, might be the least we can do for him to have even a minimally known presence on the other end."

The captain knew he wasn't going to win this one, Still, it was his call. He exhaled brusquely. "Let's get you harnessed trooper. Get the ladder over. Let's go, men."

Two minutes later they had eased the firetruck over to the edge of the embankment, settled the cleats in place and extended the ladder and basket out over the site. The basket driver got them into place and then down. Carter climbed over the edge, holding on and facing the driver. He got himself as close to the bottom edge as he could. Then he let go.

The jolt was surprisingly hard for a fall of only two feet. Once he stopped swaying he was able to steady himself into a spread-eagle, skydiving-like pose.

"Down," Carter said. "Little more. Ok. There. Stop."

Carter's head was right at the limb's top opening. He spoke into it.

To Justyn the words came across like shouts, amplified down the tree tube and into his dying space.

For Carter, he was glad of the limb's natural sound properties. The man he was trying to save could barely speak. No one else heard a word of their interaction but from a distance they could tell something basic and vital was happening. It was amazing that the trooper was even having this interchange. They waited. It felt a little like last rites.

Carter's head snapped back. "Up!"

The basket driver fumbled the controls.

"Up! Now!"

His urgency caught everyone by surprise.

"Swing him back," the captain yelled, forgoing the previous safety measure of getting him back in the basket.

The massive arm moved the trooper out and away from the center and over to the edge, depositing him into the snow. He rolled over, still harnessed in as Bradford hurried over.

"What?! What happened. Alive? What did he say?"

"Glad to fill you in on all we talked about later. But we gotta go. What time is it?" he scrambled out of the harness.

"Hold on, Jons. It's about 4:15. Why? And where are we going?"

"Omaha. CHI Health Arena."

FORTY THREE

"He gonna make it?"

Bradford's voice came across Carter's bluetooth as they headed away from the old farm road.

Conditions were slightly better but the road was still slick. The snow clearing equipment had moved much of the material to the sides but then flattened it as they went, creating a more packed but slipperier drive.

"I really don't know. He was so weak. I mean, c'mon. Three days?"

They got back out onto G61 and headed west, away from McClelland and toward Council Bluffs.

"You mind filling me in on the rest of it? At least, why we're heading to Omaha? You realize that makes no sense, right, Jons? Care to also let me in on why, if we are so urgently heading there, we have not called anything in yet?"

"Just give me a few more minutes, Bradford. Thinking. I just need a few minutes. I know it's asking a lot, but follow me. Please, just follow me."

He signaled and then turned.

"Jons?"

"Just, please, Bradford."

She turned as well, knowing the direction they were going was neither back to District or Omaha, at least for the moment.

The two cruisers made their way past a few strip malls and then down one-way streets. A playground and a school. A tree-lined neighborhood, definitely older homes. Well-kept for the most part. Carter pulled into a driveway and then alongside the house, to a back parking lot by a medium- sized garage posing as a workshop. The snow had been cleared recently but was piling up again, encroaching on the paved open space.

He got out, headed for the back door, motioning for Bradford to follow suit.

"Babe? That you?"

Mae's head turned from what she was doing and she walked over as Carter took his parka and hat off.

"Whoa, CJ. You look like you've been through it."

Bradford walked in.

Mae composed herself and took a step, establishing her territory without a word. Not aggressive, just an understanding. Ground rules.

"Come in," she offered. "Amy? Trooper Bradford?"

"Thank you ma'am. Yes, I'm Trooper... Amy." She shot Carter a look, giving him no more leash without an explanation.

"Mae? Kids?"

"Playing upstairs. Sounds like they didn't hear you coming in yet."

"That's good. I could use your thinking for a minute, too."

They headed into the living room, Bradford hesitant to sit until Mae insisted.

"Jons," Bradford started. "I'm pretty much done here. Talk."

"Okay. Justyn was really struggling to speak."

"Justyn?" Mae asked.

"The van with changed plates," she deserved some context. "We found it. Buried in a snowbank, down by a creek bed. Old farm road outside McClelland."

That was enough for Mae to get up to speed. "Got it, go on. Justyn."

"I get a few seconds with him. Not much. Not that lucid. Then he clear as day says *Omaha*. Then *arena*. And then he gets out *7pm*."

"Jons," Bradford stepped in. "That got cleared this morning. ATF. HomeSec. Bureau. We all had assignments on our side and they came back clear, too."

Mae took in that piece of info, knowing even more now how her husband's day had gone. She looked at Carter. "Anything else?" She could tell he was holding something back about their interaction, something important but not necessary to their current dilemma. "From Justyn?" she clarified.

"Two more words. First one, he said it three times. Each one got a little more desperate."

The two women waited.

"*Go.*"

Carter paused.

Mae leaned forward.

"*Bomb.*"

"It's almost five now," Bradford cut back in. She'd taken off her gloves at the door but only as she looked at her watch did Mae see her fingertips. She closed her hands, covering them.

"But you get why this is not an easy call, right?" Carter probed.

"Yeah, I do," Bradford processed. "All we have is the urgency of a dying, likely homegrown terrorist. The van is circumstantial. Intriguing but not damning. Even if we can get it out of there and find what… explosives, or materials? That would take days."

"I don't like the play up the chain," Carter added. "You think shift sarge, let alone district lieutenant is gonna move it forward? I mean, okay, say they did. Are any of the agencies gonna believe it's as critical as we think? Let's assume Justyn was supposed to be there tonight to do some very bad things. He gets waylaid for three days."

"He was under snow for three days?" Mae said.

"Yeah," Carter acknowledged. "Pretty amazing. So this morning's alert was for another guy entirely. Perry Townsend. Was he half the materials? Supposed to meet Justyn?"

"Or maybe a replacement for Justyn?" Mae offered.

"Exactly," Carter answered. "We don't know. And that would mean maybe there's even someone else involved that we don't know about."

"I get it, Jons, I get it. We act now. But there's still one big issue that we can't get around."

"I know. But we can't just let jurisdiction be the closed door here. Best case scenario: we go, find nothing and nothing happens."

"Yeah, but there's a pretty bad worse case, too. And what do you think is gonna happen the second a couple of Iowa State Troopers show up across state lines in Nebraska and demand to… what, are we going in to search, seize? Evacuate? There's likely half of the ten thousand attendees already there. Maybe more."

"Have no idea, Bradford. Besides one simple fact. Not going in as Iowa State Troopers."

Mae saw where this was headed and motioned Bradford to follow. "Yeah, you're about my size."

Mae pulled out a few options.

Bradford mulled them over. All were casual, fairly loose fitting. Running shoes. She liked how this woman was thinking. Her eyes caught a few items around the room. Asian decor. Much of it seemed very personal. Family.

Mae noticed. "Vietnamese," she explained. "Third generation in the States. Grandparents were in business. Good life for themselves and my mom. Viet Cong took everything. Reassigned them to a work camp. They ran, at night. Barely made it out in time and barely made it to San Fransisco, months later."

"That's quite impressive, Mrs. Jons."

"Yeah, wasn't easy from there, either. Harder than they thought to achieve again only a portion of what they'd had back home. And they had their fair share of stupid people making things more difficult than need be. Even then, not many places in the world you can rebound. Rebuild like that. I mean, not that easy for me, either. I've met a lot of idiots, too. Some, downright cruel. As you've probably figured out by now, mom met a nice guy from the community. Old country. Culture. They mostly stuck together. Didn't think they'd be able to have kids after a while. But years later, here comes Mae Mae."

Bradford stopped, taking in Jons' life and family with the new data points.

"Amy," Mae slowed her words. "He's a good man. Make sure I get him back in one piece, okay?"

"Hey," Carter walked in. "We need to move it. Uh…," seeing his wife's clothes on Bradford, "that's a little weird."

"Carter Jons," Mae said. "You'd better get out of here before I come to my senses and stop this whole thing. I'll be praying. And it's a good thing you've got her with you," she smiled.

The two troopers in plain clothes slipped their service weapons along their beltlines, put on civilian hats and coats, and headed out the back door.

FORTY FOUR

Thankfully the streets were clear.

Carter's home to the arena had taken just under thirty minutes. Their Dodge Caravan made for an unassuming approach. And once he explained all its quirks with heating, seats, and door latches, it provided a fine ride from A to B.

They pulled the parking voucher from the dispenser and the gate went up. Carter tossed it onto the dash.

"Tickets?"

"Yeah, in your email. But I think we just squeezed in. Website was super slow on my phone and I don't think it was the phone. Did you know she was going to be here tonight?"

"Huh?" carter wheeled around another level of the garage.

"Senator Hicks. It's pretty much the entire homepage for the conference. I don't recall that as part of our briefing this morning."

"Ah, me either. But that was their side of the alert. Not surprised they kept it… *brief.*"

"Don't do that again, Jons," she groaned. "Ever. Or I might just have to tell Mae there was an unfortunate accident. I did my best, really, Mrs. Jons…"

Carter nodded, pride of pun a dad-thing. He also became slightly uneasy at the thought of Mae and Bradford teaming up on him at some point. Coming into the room while they were working on her cover, it had felt... what? Not necessarily friendly. At least not overtly so. Maybe just a growing respect? They were, after all, two pretty impressive people.

5:30pm.

Carter and Bradford had their digital tickets scanned and walked into the giant atrium space. So much glass and light. The place was buzzing. Booth after booth lined the outside perimeter. Manned by mostly young, very eager men and women, faces shining with purpose. Sport events and concerts were one thing. There's always fan loyalty and if something big is on the horizon — playoffs, album drops — an extra measure of excitement can appear for a while. But the energy of most gatherings ends there. This was something different. Everyone here was giving themselves to something bigger *than* themselves. Sure, there was a wide range of issues. And a reasonable array of solutions. But make no mistake, these thousands were here for reasons beyond entertainment or fame. To them, the world was brimming with possibility as long as humans walked the planet. Every age, every generation was making progress. It was inevitable. You could see it in their slogans. Whatever the societal ill, they were not just addressing it. They were straight up promising, given the right resources and brainpower, that they would be eliminated. In our lifetime. No longer weighing down life on earth. It was full-chested humanistic, scientific and moral triumphalism. And it was heady.

"You catching the same vibe?" Bradford asked.

"Nothing a history book or two can't douse, but yeah, it's powerful."

"There you go again. Why would you want to stop this," she looked around.

"Hey," Carter sidestepped the conversation. "We've got a limited time horizon here. If you were going to," he lowered his voice. "Bring this place down. Probably not up here, right?"

"No. Think about how the pros do it. Demolitions are usually a series of charges, not one big one. It's the cumulative effect kind of thing. With a heavy reliance on mass and gravity to make it all happen."

"Agreed."

Both walked over to a door marked "stairwell." Bradford tried the knob. Locked. They heard footsteps on the other side and slid behind a large concrete column.

Buzz.

Click.

A man in overalls came out and then stepped away, toward some other equipment or food service emergency.

Carter's toe caught the door. He nudged it open a little then pushed it forward. Bradshaw followed. The door closed behind them. He pointed and they descended.

Level Sub1.

The door at the bottom was unlocked on the inside. They could proceed but would need a similar happenstance if heading back up at some point. Neither thought that likely. Carter opened the door and then took a couple steps. They'd have to be careful and ready to lie, act, or both. Carter suggested autographs. The conference band had quite the merch table in the atrium and they didn't want to wait in line?

"That could work for me, maybe," she'd said. "But, what's the old white guy hanging around for?"

In the end, they had to settle on the truth. Well, partial truth. Plan A was to not be noticed or questioned as to their presence in the service areas of a large arena, hosting some ten-thousand people in the seats above. Plan B? Badges. They were Iowa State Troopers in plain clothes, tasked as part of the enhanced security measures for the senator's surprise appearance. Upside was they could sell that very convincingly. Downside: they were cops. And their presence could alert the very person or persons they were looking for. Or maybe they weren't even looking for perps at this late stage. Maybe all had been set in motion and they were only trying to uncover the explosives before it was too late. And what then?

"I'm assuming you have as much explosives and ordinance expertise as me," Carter mentioned.

"Green wire," she said. "Just don't ever cut the green wire."

He stopped walking.

"Jack Bauer? 24? Never, *ever* cut the green wire, Jons."

Her deadpan was perfect and it did relieve some tension for a moment.

"You watched?… "

"Ever heard of YouTube, rookie? Anything and everything. Watched a few episodes with my dad. Hooked."

It became apparent Plan A would be near impossible to engage for the long haul. Just too many people down here. Conference volunteers running papers and boxes and people from place to place. CHI Health staff doing their thing. Vendors everywhere. Deliveries were coming in and through the gates just outside, every few minutes. Carter and Bradford did their best, but at some point slinking from behind gray column to another gray column was going to draw more attention than not.

"Badges?" Carter asked.

"Badges."

FORTY FIVE

It had taken three more hours to find the bad connector.

O nce located, Richards and Townsend made quick work of the replacement. It was, after all, a series of electric switches. Not unlike a string of Christmas lights. But in this case, the old kind where a single fault caused enough interference to stop the flow. The problem lay somewhere among sections 116-123. Checking each twenty-foot section manually was laborious. Neither man had anticipated being here this close to the event. And neither wanted to be here any longer than necessary.

"More tests?" Townsend whined.

"Yes, more tests. They all check out locally now. But that was the case before, too. Conductivity along the entire run needs to be confirmed. And what are you all up in arms about? I thought this was the big victory for you and your *people*."

"Well, yeah, it is."

One level above them crowds poured in. Excited voices. Another section of seating had opened. Quickened footsteps. Anticipation.

Perry looked up.

"What?" Richards saw it. "You having problems with what we're doing here?"

"No, no. I just," words were getting stuck.

224 WAYNE C STEWART

"You're pathetic. You know that don't you?" he took his cap off, resetting as he scratched his forehead with the inseam. "Or what, they told you you were important? Saved you somehow? Oh, that's it. You owe them this. Or at least you think you do."

"Shut up!" Townsend stepped forward. So much had gone wrong. He'd made so many mistakes. This whole thing was nothing at all like he imagined. But he'd already crossed the line. More than once and in more than a few different ways.

Richards laughed. The man was so callous. "You don't even see it." He looked up toward renewed sounds from above. "Me? I'm doing this because of what it will get me. But, you? You're doing this because," he pointed up "… of who they *are.* I long ago learned to live with a job well done. Not sure you can as easily live with your hate."

"Hey, you guys MidTown Digital?"

Perry looked over, catching a slight flash of Richards' gun, still at his waist.

"Yeah," Richards offered, coming down from his ladder. "What you need? We're on a pretty tight schedule here."

"Yes," the man with the clipboard said. "And we're the ones paying you to keep that schedule."

Perry looked over and saw the lanyard badge: *CHI Health Staff.*

"They need you backstage."

"*Who* needs us backstage?"

"Audio-visual contractors. Something about your new lines not supplying the clarity you claimed. Or something like that," he trailed off, looking for the next item on his list.

"We don't work with AV, just power and signal."

"Well, they say it's your problem. You say it's theirs. We just need you to fix it."

Richards begrudgingly made his way to the staging area. He approached the tech lead.

"You guys can't figure out your own systems?"

"Nice," the lead returned. "Thanks, cable man. Look, we're not getting anywhere near the throughput you promised. Check out the meters yourself. We need this fixed yesterday. What is it with you people? I told the arena folks to go with a known service. And now, here we are, less than two hours before the show. Well? What're you staring at. What you guys gonna do about it?"

Richards stared him through.

The man took a step back.

"Like I said. It's not our problem. As in, our systems are not causing the problem. Not that I should get involved, but what converters are you running? Look at your graphs. That low end of the digital spectrum analysis. I've seen better from a first year comp sci geek trying to boost a Nintendo 64."

The AV guy took another look. He wouldn't face Richards but he made a few keystrokes and then adjusted some settings on a manual control surface.

The CHI Health lanyard guy walked up and glanced at the massive screens. "Ok. See what happens when everyone plays nice?"

"Let's try this again."

Richards pulled up the app from inside his van, parked near Section 123.

Townsend watched.

Section 101 lit green. 102. 103. 104. 105. 106…

Solid green flashed across that entire side of the arena, 101-110.

Richards started the test for the opposite side. 116, green. 117. 118. 119…

Another flash of solid green for 116-125.

"See? No worries."

The man repeated the tests three more times for each side. Satisfied, he tapped open another tab, this time a basic web control page. It hosted a digital clock, levers with each of the sections on them, and then one more, single button. Richards checked the time on his phone.

5:43pm.

He flipped the separate onscreen switches for each of the sections holding their device. Text appeared over each.

Armed.

At section 101 a very small box lit up with a single activity light. And again at 116.

He typed in 7:20pm and hit "set." A similar piece of text floated over the entire screen.

Live.

More and more people were walking around upstairs, taking their seats. The band had begun its final sound check. Booming low end, cheers, and clapping resonated through the concrete structure. The conference had made a superfan agreement for early-access tickets. Nearly a thousand paid the extra seventy-five dollars.

Townsend looked to the ceiling again. "That it?"

"Almost," Richards said, pulling his sidearm.

Townsend shouted and his left arm came up reflexively, shaking the van seat and skewing Richards' aim.

The gun fired.

Townsend slumped against the door.

Richards drove fifteen feet forward, to where more construction debris was stored. He ran around the other side, opened the door, and Townsend fell out. He was just about to pull the trigger again when he heard a service vehicle making its way toward them, down the maze of tunnels. Instead, he quickly dragged Townsend over and behind the massive piles of sheet rock and tarps. Pulling one over Perry, he got back in his van, wiped down the window, and then drove casually toward the exit he'd come into earlier that day. He waved. Security lifted the gate and he pulled out. Before turning onto 10th street and then the interstate, he opened his specialized camera app and set his phone into its dashboard cradle. It would be another ninety minutes before the signal came on, showing the unobstructed view from atop the *Omaha Hilton*. He'd be well on his way by then. Still, he didn't want to miss it.

FORTY SIX

Carter and Bradford moved throughout the arena's subterranean corridors.

"Way easier if we just jumped on stage and stopped this thing."

Bradford agreed, at least strictly speaking. "But that would presuppose we find something worth stopping the conference for."

"True," Carter replied. "Don't get me wrong. Would way prefer to find nothing. And then also that there was nothing to find. Maybe this plot failed twice. Justyn and then Townsend. That would be fine by me. We can sneak away unnoticed, head home, and call it a very weird day. And then these people can just have a nice time doing their conference thing."

"Leaves a murderer on the loose," Bradford summed.

"We'll have to let that play out in other jurisdictions."

"For sure. And say we do find something," she replied. "Getting on stage won't be easy. Senator's security team? Probably not in a great mood."

Carter nodded. After the morning's threat level alert and then all-hands-on-deck search, they would likely shoot first and maybe not even get to asking questions later. "Agreed. No bomb. No problem. Bomb? That just starts up a whole other set of problems."

They kept to a brisk walking pace. Even with badges out they wanted to appear as much a part of the landscape as possible. Enhanced security should look like they meant business. Play the part. Keep your eyes open.

The two rounded a corner and the floor sloped gently. A bank of elevators opened on their right. Every few seconds two or three people came out and pushed empty carts over to a prep area, where mountains of food and hospitality supplies sat, staged and ready for transfer to numerous options at the first two levels. About fifteen feet to their left was a separate pile. Different options. Catered and box suites would get these.

Bradford looked past and over to enormous loading bays.

"What a nightmare," she breathed. "How many bad guys or things could come in through there?"

It all looked so normal from any other perspective. And it was actually quite impressive. Logistics were not her area of expertise but she knew a well-run operation when she saw it. Seemingly little waste of energy or time. Carts moved past one another flawlessly. Loaders packed efficiently. Ants in a colony. Everyone had their job and was doing it well. For the good of the whole.

"Anything?" Carter asked.

"Nope. At least nothing that sticks out, right? Which is exactly how a bad actor would want it to appear."

"One committed party."

She reflected on their training. "Could be any one of them. Or a few. Or none."

Carter thought he had read that idea somewhere before encountering it in their coursework. Maybe a book or a History Channel special. But it had hit home for real when a federal protective services agent admitted it. Surveillance. Intel. Onsite forces in numbers. You could get the sharpest, bravest people involved and still not be able to thwart an attack from a single, committed individual. Add some kind of principled fuel to their fire and it became even more of a crap shoot. It had happened more than once in American history. All the more reason for vigilance. And to celebrate the wins when they came.

Bradford thought the same things but on a deeper level. She hoped to transfer soon from Trooper Two to Trooper One, assigned to capital duties in Des Moines, and from there the governor's protection detail. The lone assailant challenge was something she had thought about often.

Moving on from the beehive of loading activity they entered a narrower passageway, wide enough for small vehicles and the ever present golf-cart type conveyances. The sounds of busy people faded. They became more aware of their new surroundings. Storage and construction. Piles of materials. Some out in the open. Others strewn about where they were last needed for a multiplicity of projects. The physical plant team for a place like this must be busy all the time.

The van sat alongside an interior wall.

Carter saw it first. He looked around, up and down the hallway. No workers. "That seem a little odd to you?"

"Maybe."

They walked over, peering into the front seat. Not much there but some paperwork.

Bradford tried the cargo hatch. "Locked."

Carter looked her way and then off into the distance. "Would be great to take a quick peek in… "

Smash.

Bradford broke the driver's side window with a small piece of concrete, left by the wall. She reached in, unlocked the door, and then pulled the cargo latch release from under the seat.

Carter smiled. "That escalated quickly."

"Hmm. Ok," she looked at the van side again, "MidTown Digital. What are you guys up to today?"

They pulled out a coiled section of cabling and straightened it on the concrete floor. About twenty feet long. Six inches around. Plastic connector caps, presumably to extend the run.

"This one looks busted," Bradford noticed. "The end cap. Looks like it was pried off, prongs bent. Seems like this came off quick and ugly."

"Well" Carter remarked. "Lots of stress around here earlier. Seems like you'd bring extras on a job like this, right?"

Bradford looked up and around, spotting the install.

"There. The column over 116."

Carter saw a flashlight in the back of the van and grabbed it. Walking over toward the column, he shined it upward, into the nest of cabling.

"That seems weird," Carter said, fumbling the flashlight trying to take a picture with his phone.

"What're you seeing?" she walked over and joined him.

"Can you get the light back up there for me? Camera flash won't throw that far," he handed it over. "Great, thanks. There's what looks like an older set of cables. It's all caged up, like you'd expect from an IT install or a cold room full of servers."

Bradford looked too, and then shined the light another few feet of the run. "Yeah, MidTown's install looks very different. That casing. Could be some kind of insulation?"

"Sure, I guess so. But I'm more concerned with that," he gestured.

She focused the beam up and into the mass of wires closest to the first level seating deck supports.

"I'm no expert, for sure," Carter continued. "But why would you need a little box at the start of a cable run? Signal amplification of some kind? Why don't the older ones have it?"

Bradford took some steps laterally, tracing the run along Section 116.

Carter caught up to where she was now shining the light overhead.

"Same connectors," she observed, "about every twenty feet, like we saw back at the van. But no little boxes. Just the one."

They walked past 116 and onto 117. The pounding of feet and music from the soundcheck bled through.

"I am not sure what we're looking at here, Jons, but think about this structurally for a second."

"Yeah, not good," he sped up. "Not good at all."

Their steps hastened as they kept the beam overhead. 117 looked much the same as the previous section. MidTown's wiring run connected end to end, spanning the sections alongside the older, more traditional cabling.

118. 119.

They started running.

120. 121. 122. 123.

FORTY SEVEN

"This is it."

Dennis looked around the room.

"In some ways, I can't believe it. Amazing. You're all amazing. The next day and a half are the culmination of so much work, so much effort. But, more than that. It's about passion. About love."

Smiles. A few tears, caught by fingertips, trying to keep mascara from running.

"Can we hear it for Dr. Paulsen?" came from the back.

A round of applause. Whistles.

"No," his hand went up. "No one person gets the kudos. Community is what matters. Solidarity on the things that matter. I know you've heard it before. Maybe so many times it's gotten old. But you, you are the generation. Gotten your heads clear. Seen the dead end of materialism and the roadblocks to equity that other generations, mine included, have not owned up to. You are the ones that will save *us*. And while many still can't see it we are now more than ever committed to doing whatever it takes to move progress forward. No more excuses. You are world changers, my friends. Nothing less than world changers."

The weight of it all sat for a moment. No one wanted to move away too quickly. This gathering, these people. History books would recall it as pivotal. They were as sure of it as anything in their lives to date.

"Well, " Dennis transitioned perfectly. "There is still work to do, right? Including… " he scanned a list, "… trash monitoring."

They laughed.

"We don't want anything to get in the way of the messages our attendees will be encountering during their brief stay with us," he finished. "No distractions."

A few minutes later the remaining tasks had been doled out. The energy was unbelievable, even among those who had fallen upon garbage duty. They left with purpose on their faces, in their stride.

"Ben? Terri?" he called out, and also a few others by name.

The small group circled up.

"How are our volunteer captains doing?"

"Great," a young woman answered. "Good folks. They're new to me, but man they're some solid leaders. Organized. Sharp. Really sharp."

Dennis was never more glad he had built that email list at every opportunity. His website. Speaking engagements. Book sales. "Most are active in their own campus groups. Stellar bunch." He turned. "VIP rooms?"

"Yep. All good to go and we've got ten volunteers checking in every few minutes across the suite level. Concierge services, for sure."

"Speakers? Main stage and breakouts?"

He was assured all was well. Like a general before battle he became more and more aware of both the ever-marching clock and the character of his people and their collective preparation. It was exhilarating.

"Hey, did that AV issue get resolved earlier?" someone asked.

"Wasn't aware of any," Dennis looked around for anyone who might know more.

An undergrad student stepped in. "Some technicians were working backstage with the AV contractor earlier. Kinda tense but looked like they got it worked out. CHI Health staff… *Clipboard Chuck…*" everyone laughed, "… was there. Seemed okay with how it all turned out. Gone through all the audio and video checks last hour so we'd have heard if anything was still busted."

Dennis frowned. He wanted more assurance.

"Yeah, professor," a few more chimed in. "Chuck was *on* it."

Dennis released almost everyone. By request, Ben and Terri remained.

"Ben," Dennis spoke. "Look, I like Clipboard Chuck as much as everyone. But… "

"Glad to."

"That would be so great. Put my mind at ease. Please let me know if it's something they're concerned about over the course of the conference, would you?"

"Absolutely," Ben looked over to the wall of their ready room. A map of *CHI Health Arena* took prominence, marked with all kinds of info and notes. "Ah, okay. There," he pointed. "Best route to backstage?" he asked.

Terri glanced over. "Yep, looks best to me. Avoid all the atrium mess."

"Alright, then." Ben declared. "Section 123, stairwell, here I come."

"Terri?" Dennis waved her over as Ben left the room. "Look, I want to apologize."

She smiled. "Oh, no. Dr. Paulsen. Not at all."

"I just. I mean, we were all so out of sorts when the search happened this morning. And I was fully onboard with the conference going on, as well. I shouldn't have snapped at you like that. Especially in front of the others. You did what we needed done, even if I would have preferred a more group approach and decision."

"I am glad to help. You know that, professor. I think I connected with the senator. Maybe she sees a younger version in me, at least a little?"

"I don't doubt that at all, Terri. Which is exactly where I need you to be now. Here's the final event order for tonight. Please let the senator know how pleased we are to have her here, that we consider this such an honor. More than that. A turning point."

She was receiving final hair and makeup touches.

"We've doubled the team around the stage and throughout the main entrances to the floor seating. Revisions on your brief remarks are on your phone. Prompter is loaded and ready to go."

"How much did you shave off the details?"

"The speech, ma'am? Your bill is now mentioned in the most generic, positive, and urgent terms."

"Good. I've told you before. No one likes… well, let's just say no one needs all the nitty-gritty. A few might do the work of reading the bill. But most? They only want to know we are doing something."

She had championed that phrase more than a few times. When a nosy opposition reporter pressed. In debates. Tweets.

It's long past time we finally *did* something.

Whatever the issue, the moral angle became the precipice. There was no longer any room for good people to agree on problems but maintain divergence on solutions. Those were the old days. She liked these days better.

"When will it be up on social?"

Her COS checked his comm plan notes. "10:30 at the latest. We've got some work to do on the front and back ends and some music bed edits but we can get that done at the hotel."

"Good," she smiled. "You know as well as I do that this is the moment. We can't count on the midterms. Yes, things can change in nine months, but I am not looking past this session. We have the votes now. We have the White House, now. We have, what? Ten thousand out there, just waiting to be mobilized. No, catalyzed. You don't get moments like this. FDR knew that. Revised America."

She pivoted.

"The rest of the evening? And tomorrow?"

"All set, madam senator. We'll be to your hotel by 7:45 tonight. Depart Eppley Field private strip precisely at 8am."

She was already there in her mind. The few hours she'd spend in this wintry stop were more than enough. A week in Bahamian paradise should set her back on balance. But then, a return to DC was only a small upgrade to Nebraska. It was still a long way until spring.

Terri stood at the doorway, waved through by a large man with a sidearm and overly obvious earpiece.

One of the staffers saw Terri enter.

"Final schedule for the senator, in case she'd like to engage the conference's other conversations."

The staffer took it.

Terri smiled knowingly, having just heard the senator's last remarks before entering the room.

"Oh, Terri, right?" the senator pulled her makeup bib off and stood. "Thank you. Thank you for all you've done here. You and your team have been excellent hosts."

"Really," Terri replied. "It's our honor. Your staffers have my cell if you need anything. Anything at all."

The senator's smile faded as the young woman left the room.

Terri walked a few feet down the hall. Slowing by a trash can, can she dropped into it the very phone just mentioned. She looked at the wayfinding signs in the conference room hallway. Following the numbers, she stopped at a doorway.

Section 123, stairwell.

FORTY EIGHT

"Stop."

"W hat?" Carter asked.
"You hear that?"
Footsteps above them had increased ten-fold in the last few moments. They'd hardly heard the shift, following the lines of cabling over the course of a few hundred feet. But now, Bradshaw heard something else.

"Kinda hard to hear anything. Sounds like the band is warmed up, though. And the crowd. That's for sure."

"Back," she pointed. "Over there."

They walked a few steps. A leg was sticking out from under a construction tarp. It was moving, twitching.

"Bradford," Carter ordered. "Help me get this off. The sheetrock. Over there, weighing it down."

The two of them flung the 8x8 sheets aside. Another leg, then a torso. Head, arms. The plastic covering came off. The man was white as a sheet. He was having a hard time breathing. The pool of blood beneath and around was enormous.

Bradford moved closer.

The man had prosthetic hair hanging off his real hair. Glasses had fallen off and cracked. A mustache dangled from where it had been pasted.

Carter pulled up the earlier alert pics on his phone. "Townsend. It's Townsend. Can you talk?" he approached the failing man. "Look, we've got to know if these people are in danger. We'll do everything we can to help you."

"We saw some very strange wiring, Mr. Townsend," Bradford said.

He was gurgling.

"All around the arena. Under the seating blocks level 1. Can you nod your head? Is that the bomb?"

His eyes glassed.

"Is *that* the bomb?!" she shot out again.

Townsend coughed and lurched to the side. Then he rolled back over. He made every effort to control his movements, to be clear even though his nerve endings were a mess. He looked Bradford in the eye. Then he nodded his head as far forward as he could. One motion. Unmistakable.

Perry was going fast. He mouthed words but the fluids were building up in his airway. Again, he rolled himself on his side. For a brief second, the troopers heard more articulate efforts.

Carter got his ear down close to a dying man for the second time today.

"Ends… ennnnds. Ughhh."

"Townsend. Ends? What ends?"

"Ennnnnds…. areeee…nuh….saaafe."

The death rattle settled. Townsend's stare fixed.

"Ends of the arena?" Bradford processed. "Maybe this ring-bomb doesn't go all the way around the seating? I think he just told us where to get everyone for their best shot at surviving this thing."

"Okay, great. But what if we don't have enough time? I mean, isn't there supposed to be a big red timer somewhere?"

"Yeah," Bradford joked. "Right next to the green wire."

"What's going on? Oh my goodness, is he okay?"

His lanyard read *Event Staff: Ben.*

"Back up, son." Bradford ordered. "Iowa State Troopers. Keep your hands where I can see them."

"I… I'm just one of the conference team leaders. Oh my gosh. He's dead, isn't he?"

Carter moved over quickly, checking Ben for weapons or anything else that would only make their lives more difficult.

"He's clean," Carter said, as Ben finally breathed again, getting greener by the second. "I'm calling in."

"Got it," Bradford replied, keeping an eye on Ben as he vomited into a trash can nearby.

"District 3 dispatch, this is Jons. We have an emergency evacuation scenario here at CHI Health Arena. We've found a… best way to describe it is a ring-bomb, running under the seating structure of Level 1. We believe there are safe zones at the far ends of the stadium and will be getting people out as quickly as we can."

"District 3 dispatch. Handing over to shift sergeant. Jons? I'm pretty sure I caught most of that, but first: why are you in *Omaha*?"

"Please, sir. We don't have time. Well, we don't know how much time we have. Justyn led us here. We discovered suspicious wiring runs and then we found Townsend. Shot, bleeding out. He's dead but confirmed it was the bomb. Sending you pictures now," he tapped a few times.

"Jons. Slow down. Justyn? The kid buried by McClelland? You sure on all this?"

"Sir, with all respect, do those wiring runs look normal to you? And yes, Justyn under all that snow for three days. And yes again, it was definitely Townsend."

Shots rang out in the enclosed space, reporting off the hard surfaces.

Terri approached, drawing down on the area the three were occupying and moving her arm slightly every second or so. Her eyes were set. She was steady.

"What?!" Ben shouted. He was so confused.

Carter and Bradford stood still. Both had drawn their weapons as well, not giving ground but neither provoking her to turn on Ben.

"You followed me?" Ben was trying to create any reasonable world in which this could be true.

"Never liked you. Certainly don't trust you. And if we're going to win today, you seemed like a potential loose end."

"Wait," Bradford called out. "Just, stop. *We*? Who in the world is 'we'."

"Look," Carter ordered. "You're not going to survive this. You really need to put the gun down. We'll get you out of here with everyone else. Arrested. But alive."

"Oh, you've got to be kidding me," she looked over at Townsend's limp, lifeless frame. "What do they say about sending the pros? Even they can't be counted on to do their job."

In one swift move she kicked up a loose pile of dust and cardboard. Then she rotated toward Bradford, sizing her up as the more serious threat.

The trooper moved her finger from side position onto the trigger. Bradford was fast, very fast, but today's hours in the cold had brought her hands to near frostbite. The minor tissue damage and soreness slowed her a fraction of a second. It was enough.

A single bullet left Terri's gun.

Bradford spun and fell.

Carter cleared his eyes of the dust and Terri was already ten yards away. He fired and missed. He fired again as she disappeared down the long interior of the arena.

"Bradford!" He yelled, racing over and past Ben, who was facedown but okay. He saw her wound, upper right arm. There wasn't much blood and she was already stanching it with her hand. Still, she was wincing as she sat back up.

"Whoah, Bradford. Just sit tight. Wait a second."

"We don't have a second."

"Sure we do."

"No, Jons, we don't. We don't have any spare time, at all."

She nodded beyond him, into the pile of debris. Her fall had moved a few larger pieces of sheet rock from where Townsend originally lay when they found him. Onto the white surface was scrawled, in red, three numbers.

720.

"You think?" Carter stared.

"Looks like Townsend tried to leave a note. Should probably take a dying man at his word."

"Okay. But, what about the assailant… "

"Terri," Ben clarified. "Well, maybe. That's what she went by with us."

"Leave her," Bradford said. "We've got ten thousand people to move in… "

"Jons. Bradford. Dispatch. You still there? Shots fired?"

Carter realized he'd dropped his phone and the line was still open.

"Affirmative, dispatch. I mean, sarge. Bradford's wounded but mobile. And… "

"And?"

"You better tell everybody we got 23 minutes. I mean, everybody. We're gonna need 'em."

FORTY NINE

The band was so very loud.

Their opening set was a medley of two classic protest songs. Familiar words. Modern arrangements.

How many roads must a man walk down...

A giant wall of sound and rhythm pounded out the questions.

Yes, and how many times must the cannonballs fly...

The barrage of tones and lights carried the attendees' emotions perfectly. They were jumping, screaming, singing at the top of their lungs.

And how many years can some people exist
Before they're allowed to be free?
Yes, and how many times can a man turn his head
And pretend that he just doesn't see?

They rode the wave together, as if each one had come ready to overflow, cresting pent up anxieties, fears, hurts, cares. For many, it was their form of religious experience. Ecstasies. But unlike many other concert settings, their passions and experience were fueled only by those chemicals found naturally in the human brain.

The band finished the first song with a full thirty-second arena ending. The screams almost kept up with the sound system. Then, surprisingly, they shifted gears completely.

So on we go

His welfare is of my concern
No burden is he to bear
We'll get there

The last refrain was magical. No instruments, just ten-thousand voices united in heart and purpose.

He ain't heavy, he's my brother
He's my brother

Everyone took it in for a beat. Then, in perfect timing the opening video package came up and the lights adjusted for maximum screen viewing. The increased clarity at size was impressive. Full immersion. The package had been outsourced, more money than the committee had paid for anything ever before. But this content was crucial. It was well worth it.

During a seamless two minutes ten thousand people were connected emotionally to all they held as their calling, their life's work. Racial disparities in work environments. Incarceration rates. Policing communities of color. Race and the environment. Historic economic injustices. Humanity's gravest ills displayed in ultra high definition video and sound. The video closed with a single text scroll and the conference logo.

For such a time as this.
Justice Now: A Call to Racial Reconciliation.

"This way. There's a shortcut to backstage!"

Carter, Bradford, and Ben were on the move. They ran through hallways, over walking bridges, and then finally the seating sections behind the staging area. At the top of the last set of stairs Carter stopped them, just in time.

"You've got to be kidding me."

"She's a piece of work, that one."

"Seriously?"

Thirty rows below, Terri was motioning wildly, communicating fear while convincingly pointing up, toward them.

The senator's security detail took the bait. The man Terri was talking to called over two others. They started up the stairs.

"Well," Carter said. "It's not like getting onto the stage and grabbing a mic was going to be easy, right?"

Ben took their situation in, thought for a second, and then picked up the pace in a different direction.

"Ben? Wait."

"C'mon. You need a mic? Plan B is this way," he pointed up and into the second level of the arena's interior.

The conference host's comments were brief, as required.

"... we know you're going to come away from this gathering refreshed, invigorated, and yes, energized. So, without further ado." He turned his head to the stage right wings. "Madam Senator!"

The applause deafened.

She moved purposefully from the wings to the podium, waving, made a perfect pause and then caught the eye contact of no one in particular while making everyone feel she had connected directly with them. She was very, very good.

"First off. Can we just say 'what about that band', yeah?" she clapped along with thousands. She gave another look to where they were standing backstage. "Amazing. Love it."

She reset. A breath and a new seriousness. The prompter scrolled.

Carter, Bradford, and Ben took the last few steps and they were at the door.

Ben used his master mag strip from the back of his lanyard tag.

Buzz.

Click.

"Hey!" The CHI Health technician turned. "You're not supposed to be in here."

The broadcast room held endless monitors, mixers, and rack mount equipment. All three stepped in quickly, the door locking again behind them. The tech saw Ben's tag. And then Carter's and Bradshaw's badges.

"Jons," Bradford pointed. "The minicam." Then she addressed the tech. "You can patch that through to the screens and sound system, right?"

"Well, yeah. But…. what is going on here?"

"We've got a full emergency evacuation on our hands and only… " Carter looked at his phone. "Sixteen minutes left."

"Left before what?!"

The look from all three intruders told him it would only waste breath and time to explain.

"Open the door, now!" came a strong voice and pounding.

The tech froze.

"Look," Bradford pressed. "There's a bomb encircling the arena, under the seating on Level 1. We've got to let people know. You need to open the camera and mic and switch it to the screens and sound system. Do it."

"Senator's security! Open this door!"

"Do it!" she demanded.

He flipped several onscreen switches. An orange light came on, right below the camera and then began blinking.

"Five, four, three… " the tech counted softly.

"Well, Jons," Bradford said. "Looks like we're going to get on stage, after all."

The light went red.

The senator felt the crowd's gaze move from her and onto the big screens. Instinctively, she turned as well.

Carter produced his badge toward the lens. "Everyone, listen up."

An immediate gasp overtook the room.

"Trooper Carter Jons. Iowa State Patrol. You are in immediate danger and must evacuate the arena as quickly and safely as you can. The safest areas to exit are the ends of the stadium, behind the staging area and then opposite."

Ten thousand sets of eyes widened.

"Go. Now, please. The ends of the stadium."

Carter's feed dropped from the screens. Color bars and static remained.

In the broadcast booth the three headed toward the door with the tech close behind. They paused before opening, bracing for what lie on the other side.

Carter pushed it open, finding the three security men at the ready but with weapons at their sides.

"Trooper," the first one said. "What do you need us to do?"

Carter noticed the screens mounted in the hallway and understood their change of heart. "The senator… ?"

"More than enough people to get her out. She's already off the stage by now."

"Okay. It's absolutely critical that people get to the ends of the arena and then out. Do whatever you can to grab anybody who looks official, lanyards, vests, arena security and off-duty cops working the event. Get them moving people in the right direction."

They nodded.

"Eleven," he looked to his phone. "Eleven minutes, that's it. And it's likely already a stampede out there."

FIFTY

The streets, lots, and common areas outside CHI Health were flooding with vehicles and people.

Men and women in uniforms of all kinds directed other helpers into a hasty semblance of refuge. Lights and sirens blared. Tires screeched as they formed up, hoping they were close enough to help while far enough to escape the coming blast and debris storm. They had no idea if they were right. Many had been here only a matter of hours before. Neither realization kept them away.

The first few hundred people emerged from the south end of the arena and were ushered under the interstate. Capitol Avenue at 10th South St had been blocked for east-west traffic. Instructed to head that direction down the now-emptied street, they ran if they could, walked fast, or simply did their best to put as much distance between them and the building as possible. It was a scared, disjointed procession. Something between the start of a street race and a busy street fair scattered suddenly.

To the north, another first group were sent across Mecca drive and into Parking Lot D. They scampered through the narrow lanes, past cars, many their own, moving as far north and east as they could and generally tracking the bend of the Missouri River some hundreds of feet to their right.

Both groups met another set of officials and stopped. This was their best shot at keeping the crowd from unhelpfully dispersing while moving them to safety. Blankets and warm liquids were quickly staged, readying for necessary dispersal. A few people escaped the vague cordon and headed who knew where into the cold and darkness. Most obeyed. And then waited.

Thankfully few residential pockets abided near the arena. Omaha PD scoured their doorsteps and hallways, sending them in any and all directions away from harm.

Atop the interstate a HomeSec agent watched from where federal and state authorities had halted traffic, above the arena and a half mile back in both directions. An increasingly frightened mass of humanity streamed from the ends of the stadium. His team had all been given the countdown. He looked at his digital watch's face.

7:12.

"Keep moving. That's it. This way."

Carter marveled at the conference volunteer's calmness. Their voice was loud enough to make a difference, even from the very back where he was trying to do the same. But it was also surprisingly calm.

The crowd was not. But neither were they a herd, driven into and over one another in self preservation. For the most part they were helping each other. Holding each other up as they stumbled forward. A large group had even stopped completely, just for a second, to make sure a few folks with physical challenges were heading the right direction and in step with everyone else. Cynicism directed at their corporate joy and convictions a few minutes ago could be understood. It's easy for groups to be caught up in a moment such as that. But their actions now proved it was largely real.

Carter lost Bradford and Ben as they'd entered the swarm. "Lord, get them out, please," he whispered. He still had the CHI Health tech at his side and continued forward, a few small steps at a time.

He was headed to the south exits, maybe two- to three-thousand in front of him. If you focused just ahead, progress seemed stopped. Looking more forward they were advancing, just very methodically. It was all a bit like they would have experienced coming out of the parking lots on a normal night. A bit of gain, then feeling like they had to wait briefly. Sort of a toothpaste tube effect. Carter could sense they were being squeezed by both the building and time.

7:18.

Carter eyed the crowd in front of him. Too many, still too close to the midsections of the arena.

He looked over to the tech and then back ahead.

"Run!" he screamed. "You have to go, *now*!"

Terri came to another wall.

She looked every direction. The series of rooms and portable dividers had not led to where she thought. She, too, looked to the time on her phone's clock. Sitting down among paint cans and discarded coffee cups, she took a deep breath.

Every twenty feet the wiring encased in explosives began to hum.

The vibrations grew into shaking, a few of the clamps loosening their hold against the understructure of Level 1 seating.

101. 102. 103. 104. 105. 106. 107.

116. 117. 118. 119. 120. 121. 122.

Halfway across 108 and 123 the shaking settled into a coordinated pulse as the 80% cumulative effect of the blast potential was reached.

109. 110.

124. 125.

Richards' camera app went live.

The man was now more than a hundred miles distant, heading north and then east across I80.

The screen flashed and then settled back to focus.

Two-thirds of CHI Health Arena came crashing down onto itself. It looked as if a toddler had tired of their Lego structure and smashed it from the middle, out.

Richards smiled. Then he noticed movement at the north and south edges of the framing. So much movement. Didn't matter. He got paid for the building. And Townsend. He tapped a few times, cropping the recording's edges, before pushing send. The dark web app delivered his visual invoice, viewed and paid immediately from a mountainside great room outside of Denver.

Carter stumbled.

The air was unbreathable, everything was a dark gray. Large chunks of concrete calved from their placements, falling and making the way even more impossible. He grabbed the torn shirt of the tech, pulling him another few feet, guiding him. But where? Fires grew to the left and right. Sheared rebar swung at them from above. He couldn't be sure backwards was wrong but his body was already heading one way. Fifty-fifty.

Screams.

Shouts.

Cries for help.

He desperately wanted to do just that. But the surroundings were only allowing now for the simplest of movements.

Carter coughed and then spit the sootiness away. His eyes burned and his limbs slowed. He stopped.

To the roots of the mountains I sank down; the earth beneath barred me in forever. But you, LORD my God, brought my life up from the pit.

"I got you."

The voice was muffled by a face mask and the sound of an SCBA, wheezing oxygen.

Carter's frame was pulled along by the strong hands of two Omaha FD personnel, through more fallen structure and then a last tunnel of dark and heat.

They stopped.

"Can you walk?"

Carter took a deep breath, rasping out the chemicals and fumes. The cold evening air hit him as both shock and strength. He looked over and saw the tech, now being carried toward help.

"Yeah," he gasped. "Think so."

He rose slowly. Someone tipped his head back, pouring water over his eyes. Blinking and then opening again, he caught his first glimpses of the destruction. And then also the throngs of people who'd made it out.

"That's it," he heard. "As far back in as we can go. No one else."

The voice saw Carter's badge, still hanging at his beltline. "Iowa? Trooper," he looked closer, "… Jons?"

Carter looked over and nodded, now upright and taking his first steps.

"Have no idea why you were here in the first place. But pretty glad you were."

Carter returned a quiet *thank you*, and then a look that said the story was much more than they currently had time for.

FIFTY ONE

He didn't even get to the top step.

Mae burst from the front door and enveloped him with her smaller frame. Her interlocked fingers formed a strong ring around his midsection. She looked up and kissed his weary, greasy face.

He just took it all in. So thankful.

"CJ," she was straight up crying now. "Everything. I need to know everything, babe, but… " she leaned back into the embrace, "… you look even worse than you did earlier."

"Kids?"

"Mia knew something was up. I told her you were doing the parts of your job that require extra courage, so we prayed. She'll want to hear more from you when you can frame it up well. Theo just thought all the lights and sirens were cool. We all breathed when you called." She eyed him again. "Babe?"

Carter's body was reasonably intact. But there was an outward expression of his internal state she was seeing. His posture. His mind and heart had been through a life-changing event. More accurately a series of events and conversations. Ideas. A bit of it spilled out as he walked through the front door and into their small but warm living room. He looked over at the mantle. Photos. Memorabilia.

Mae saw him visibly shake his head as if he could just toss away the thought.

"You want to know the weirdest thing?" he asked.

"Yeah, pretty sure I'm ready for weird."

"Family."

"Ours?"

"No. Well, I mean kind of," he was able to voice it now, having thought and prayed, having lived through it. "Family. Actually *'The Family'*. HomeSec debrief this morning, we heard that's what they—the group Townsend, the original suspect in Omaha was part of—call themselves."

"That's pretty twisted."

"Agreed. But it does speak powerfully to what they were twisting."

Carter looked at the wall clock and then at his phone. No word yet from District.

"Carter," Mae ordered. "Go to bed. Your tank is all fumes. Maybe not even that."

He hesitated.

"Go."

He relented, kissed her again, and then walked toward the stairs, avoiding the creakiest boards as he went.

Ten minutes later Mae walked past their open bedroom door. Carter barely made it to their bed. Half under the sheets, his pants and shirt were still on while he'd mustered enough strength to flip his shoes a couple of inches. One sat just over the edge of the duvet. She grabbed it, picked up the other, and set them both in the closet. Then she gently laid the remaining covers over her sleeping husband.

Jefferson County- Colorado

Five squad cars and one unmarked vehicle with federal plates came to a halt.

The massive circular drive was now blocked for entry or exit as the officers took their places.

A pronouncement, then pounding. Finally the door opened. The wife assured them her husband was not home. Working late. The mill, always the mill.

The canine officer straightened, then jerked left, toward the edge of the house and the open space behind.

The detective sergeant gave the order.

Her handler/partner loosed her and the pursuit was over within seconds.

"Release!"

The man writhed in pain, grabbing at his lower right leg.

Three deputies came to an abrupt stop in the snow. They drew down as the detective sergeant and bureau agent stepped forward. The officers cuffed him and set him onto his knees.

"Ahhhh," he let out. "You can't… you have no… this is private property!" his shouts echoed off the vast meadow and into the mountainside.

They ignored it, knowing his wounds would be attended in a few moments.

The DS yielded to the agent. She smiled back.

"… you are under arrest for conspiracy to commit mass murder and conspiracy to commit domestic terrorism under 18USC 2331-5. You have the right to remain silent… "

A few moments later the suspect's head was lowered as he got into the back of the unmarked car. Then the door shut.

"Sergeant," the agent from the Denver field office started. "You and your team made this happen. Thank you."

"Glad to be of help. But it seems more like we both had what each other needed on this."

She nodded, appreciative again that the screen version of law enforcement turf wars was, most of the time, merely that.

The DS's face formed a question.

She stopped. "Terrorism charges?"

"Yeah, not my area. Got enough to make that stick?"

"Yes, sergeant, I think we do. And the two other arrests... heard they came off without trouble, will only help. Ideologically-motivated criminals tend to stick together. The evidence is enough, already. Still, someone's going to talk, sooner or later. Only makes for a stronger conviction, in the end. Sarge?" she asked. "Heard you were Philly? Glad we had someone here with a little more experience on the gritty side."

"Yeah," he laughed. "Go to the mountains, they said. It'll be quiet there. Traffic stops. A few drunk and disorderly's, they said. Somebody lied, big time."

"Well," she laughed through her slowly closing door. "Just keep up the good work."

Council Bluffs, Iowa

Carter woke suddenly, tried to focus, forcing himself more conscious and clear.

Mae sat at the end of the bed, riveted to the tv on the wall.

"I'm so sorry, CJ. You were so out. But I knew you'd want to see this."

He looked around, grasping for any sense of the time.

"Eleven-forty," she supplied.

No wonder he felt so groggy. Had probably just entered a REM phase. He sat up, raked his hands across his face and took a deep breath. He coughed. While the medics had been so good they said the smoke was going to take a while to clear out completely.

"Absolutely miraculous," the reporter was beside himself. "Officials are telling us that tonight's explosion at CHI Health Arena has yielded only two likely deaths."

The co-anchor took to her lines. "We're being told that an extraordinary effort via a conference phone app has accounted for all but the two likely fatalities. We have information for only one at this time."

The screen brought up the image of a strikingly beautiful young blond.

The female reporter continued. "Terri Roberts. If you're out there and okay, everyone wants to know it. And if any of our viewers have information about Terri's whereabouts or condition, please call the number at the bottom of the screen."

Mae looked back at Carter. He was unsurprised. That said enough for now.

"Also," the anchor pivoted. "Authorities are telling us now that the near destruction of the arena is suspected of being the work of a small domestic separatist group from Colorado, just outside the Denver metro area. Arrests have been made. More on that as it unfolds. Lastly, the surprise visit of an up and coming senator almost ended tragically. An interview with her chief of staff at the top of the hour."

Off camera, the male reporter nearly jumped. His producer was practically screaming into his earpiece.

"Sara," he stepped in. "We're cutting to a live feed… " he struggled to understand the words from the booth while keeping the conversation going. "A live feed now from the northeast edge of the Quad Cities."

Carter sat up and moved to the end of the bed alongside Mae.

A new camera shot emerged from high above the Mississippi River. A gentle bend marked this crossing at the state lines of Iowa and Illinois. The reporter came on. "Eric Theissen, here. KWQC TV6. We received word only fifteen minutes ago that authorities were converging in some manner of pursuit related to tonight's bombing in Omaha."

"I knew it," Carter said to the television. "Townsend was not the kind of guy to pull something like that off by himself."

Mae didn't stop him, letting the thought add to the unfolding drama.

The shot switched from Theissen to out and below the mostly glass airframe of the small private chopper. The entire span of the Fred Schwengel Memorial Bridge came into view.

"At this point, though," he said dejectedly. "Just a sparse line of vehicles approaching the river on I80. *Wait…* "

Carter sat forward even further.

A group of lights came on, revealing three squad cars each at both the west and eastbound exits on the Iowa side of the river, blocking those roadways. The line of regular traffic proceeded onto the bridge. Five other patrol cars pulled out from small, hidden speed traps at the structure's first few feet. Flashers announced their presence and authority. Eight cars pulled over immediately. One acted erratically, passing into and through the opposite traffic flow and then back over, speed increasing rapidly.

In much the same maneuver lights came on on the Illinois side. Five pursuit vehicles headed straight for the mid-line. They stopped and formed up sideways, as each officer took a firing position in the small space at the hinge between car door and windshield.

"A van," Theissen reported. "Smaller, white cargo van."

The vehicle stopped just shy of the Illinois State line. The driver tried backing up. Then he stopped, again.

"Pull to the side," the reporter asked his pilot.

The shot changed again, this time more level, closer. Their forward lights helped cut a little through the heavy snowfall.

The driver's side door opened. A man stepped out. Onto his knees, hands straight up, empty. Police swarmed the van and then opened the back cargo door.

"Swing around, just a little more," the reporter said.

"Yes!" Carter let out, the shot unsteady but revealing just what he wanted to know.

"From here," the reporter squinted at the small tv monitor onboard. "We can just make out a vinyl sign as the police pull it out of the cargo area. No identification on the van itself. And some kind of, what... tubing? Cables?"

Mae looked closer at the tv. "*MidTown Digital*? I'm thinking that's good?"

Carter sighed. "Very good."

His phone rang. He snatched it up.

"Uh, yes, sir... uh huh."

Mae glared for lack of data.

"Yeah, oh okay. Bradford?... Ben... the tech?" a wave of relief washed over him. "Thank, God," he whispered and then hung up.

"CJ, I'd press for details but you look like you're about to pass out. Let's make it simple. More good news?"

"Yep," he smiled. "Feds scoured CHI Health entry logs right after the explosion. Two white service vans came in today. Bradford and I reported only one, close to where we found Townsend. APB went out statewide. He almost made it to Illinois. We got him, Mae. We got him."

EPILOGUES

FIFTY TWO

TWO MONTHS LATER

ADX Florence, Federal Supermax Prison- Florence, CO

He was still recovering.

While time had passed since the crash and the three days that held him at death's door, the ravages of freezing temps still showed on his body: hands, arms, and face. Patches were healing. His legs, horribly broken by the frozen water at his ankles and the final shift of the van, would require more surgery, more therapy.

Carter had stayed away from Justyn. In part because there were legal steps, best to just stay clear. Let the process play out. But also because he was undergoing a serious effort at healing, as well. His was more internal. Carter knew the intensity of those wintry days was a gift from his Father, wanting a beloved son to grow, to change, to hear and be urged on to become more like His Son, Jesus.

The guard buzzed him in.

Carter's steps echoed on the concrete flooring. He stopped at the cell door. The young man was waiting, sitting in a wheelchair. No pictures, no posters. Not even a small tv, as was often allowed.

"Turn. Face the back wall."

He did.

The guard unlocked the door, let Carter in, and then locked it again, standing just to the side.

"You're him?"

"Yeah. Carter. Carter Jons."

"Voice sounds different."

"Well. That makes sense as I'm not usually talking through a hollow tree branch."

Nothing.

Carter decided to go for broke.

"Do you know the story of Jonah and the Whale?"

Justyn's face shifted. Surprise? At least, curiosity.

"Okay. I can see you do. Well, this may sound completely bonkers. But the day we found you? That very morning I was praying and reading that story from my Bible."

Justyn listened a little more intently. He'd had no idea why the trooper requested a visit. Had just assumed it was the same posturing, interrogations, or promises of deals he'd regularly received since being locked up.

Carter continued. "At its heart, its about heading the wrong way. But, it's more than that. The reasons Jonah was headed the wrong way were a tragic combination of who he believed he was and who he believed others were. Sadly, he lived out a very small life when God had so much more for him. And sometimes that smaller vision can become a driving force for, well, evil."

The words seemed to fall back at Carter's feet.

"Justyn. You gave me the information that Trooper Bradford and I needed. Why?"

"Not sure. It was all pretty confusing. Don't make too much out of it."

"I think that would be wrong, Justyn. You need to hear a different story about you, that you were made in the image of God and are dearly loved by Him. You've taken in one lie at a time, until the sum total is almost too much to unscramble. At the end," Carter probed. "You called out to God. Didn't you? Most people do."

"What're you, a preacher or something? Thought you were a cop."

"Well, kinda both," Carter smiled. "Justyn, I firmly believe God was speaking to both of us through that passage. And it's absolutely true that God will reach down into any kind of depths and pull out, rescue, anybody who cries out to Him. Anybody, Justyn. You. Me. Anybody. Jesus went to the cross to bear the sin and shame of all of us. And three days passed that time, too. If sin and death couldn't do Him in, then nothing can. That power is held out for anybody. It changes us forever, Justyn."

"Don't deserve it," Justyn looked up briefly.

"Nobody does."

"Trooper Carter. I appreciate you coming. Really, I do. Hits me that I should thank you. Did an awful lot to save me. Even put you and the lady cop in danger."

Carter thought he saw an opening.

"But," Justyn continued. "I don't know about all this religion stuff. Seems like it causes as much trouble as anything. I did what I did. Not proud. And I'll pay. But you can't think a few minutes of Bible stories wipe away everything. Makes me wonder, though. The probability of you even finding me was... "

"Astronomical."

"Time's up."

The serious man with the keys opened the cell door.

Carter stepped halfway through. "Hey, not your lawyer, but they offering anything at all?"

"Maybe. Dangling life no parole out there now and then. Don't know if they're serious or not. Said I might be some help in learning how people like me, well, get to be like me. Not like there's some big network I can let them in on, so I guess it's worth it to poke around in my head and maybe be able to see something in someone else."

Carter looked him in the eye. "Take it, Justyn. Take it."

Carter's nine hours home gave him plenty of time to think and pray.

Almost there, he made a surprise turn. He hadn't planned to stop. It just sort of happened. The sign at the front desk said to come on down the office hallway if no one was there. Carter noted it was a little past 5pm. Made sense. Maybe he should just turn around. Mae was expecting him by 6, anyway.

"Can I help you?" a head poked out.

"Pastor?" Carter asked. "Pastor Sam?"

Sam wiped his hand of toner from the now-opened copy machine innards and extended it as he stood. "Carter. Great to see you. How's Mae? Mia, Theo?"

Two things surprised Carter in that moment. One: he, Mae, and the kids had been attending Church at the Heights on Sundays since the Omaha incident but he'd also made sure they slipped in as the first song started and then out again as quickly as possible afterward. The church was great. The people were great. It made no sense but he was still on guard, even a little. The church was huge compared to the one Carter had led, so it struck him that Sam made the easy and quick association in this moment. It was likely the pastor had heard about the rookie trooper's role in the events, but still it made a difference. He was being gently known, welcomed at his own pace. Second, though, Carter was caught off guard that the man would have toner on his hands. Didn't he have staff for that? They could at least afford a service contract. He'd seen the budget numbers.

Sam saw the confusion.

"Summers during seminary," he filled in. "Worked for a print and production business. Learned how to take them apart and mostly put back together again. Let me tell you a little secret about ministry."

Carter was certain the man knew nothing of his former vocation.

"People," Sam started. "Super complex and never finished. But this machine here," he motioned. "Reasonably simple and repairable. I mean, except for the software side of things. Would have no idea how to get at that. Anyways, every now and then, when most of what I do is deal in complexities and unfinished work, it's nice to just replace a screw here or there and, *voila*," he shut the copier door and it booted back up, pulling a perfectly aligned test page out onto the tray. "Yeah," he said. "That looks pretty good."

"It does," Carter agreed.

"But," Sam leaned in. "Once I fix something like this, I am ready to get back to what they actually pay me for around here. Carter?"

"Pastor?"

"Maybe you came in today with some complexities and unfinished business? We haven't had the chance to talk yet. If you're up for it, I've got a thermos filled with a great Ugandan roast in my office. Would you like to talk, Carter?"

Carter breathed out, emotion taking him by surprise. "Pastor, I'd like that. I'd like that very much."

FIFTY THREE

Carter's shift had been uneventful.

He wasn't mad about it.

Speeding tickets, equipment failures, tonnage overruns. He could do that all day, every day, even the trucker with the foul mouth and complete misunderstanding of motor vehicle law. It's not like he didn't have options. In the aftermath of Omaha the governor quietly invited him to consider moving to Trooper 1 at the Capital in Des Moines, maybe even a spot on her protective detail. But he was a rookie, after all, so that would be at least two years down the road. She had re-election in three, so it could work. He kept the personal letter from the governor to himself and Mae, promising to pray over it in the coming months. For now, regular road duty was just fine by him.

The weather was moving in the right direction, too. The white that covered streets, rooftops, and fields now gave way to the browns and emerging greens of spring. Mountains of ice-packed snow, set into place by massive Department of Transportation gear, still stood at most intersections and parking lots. But its time was limited. Less freeze and more thaw made sure of that.

Carter grabbed his jacket, said goodnight to the troopers on shift, and headed down the hallway. The dribbling sound caused him to stop.

"Hey, how's it feeling?"

Bradford looked up from the half court, near the three-point line. "Not bad. A little sore. Range of motion is almost back to where it should be."

"PT?"

"Yeah, don't get me started, Jons. Bunch of medieval torture specialists, that bunch." She turned and shot. One smooth motion and the ball hit the bottom of the net.

Carter whistled.

She took two steps and caught the ball on its second bounce, passed it a couple of times through her legs and then drained another from a swift post move. Bradford caught the ball again.

Carter was still there.

He'd been trying to have this conversation, or some form of it, since before their hasty partnership in and around McClelland. One would think that being forced into life and death circumstances would forge a bond, cover over relational crevices. No. While he thought maybe there was a thinning of the ice, it's not like everything had warmed between them, even two-plus months later.

"Bradford?" he decided to go for broke.

She saw the look.

"So, about Pleasanton."

Her pause gave him the slightest opening.

"I still can't believe it. I mean, I absolutely believe it. I just know I shouldn't be surprised, either. It was horrible. Evil. And what we just ran into? Yeah, makes me think a little harder, for sure. But I also read up on the stats again. Even the stuff not constituting

enforceable crime. I hope the numbers tell us we're leaving some —
a lot — of that behind."

"Look, Jons," she held the ball for a second and stopped. "Like I
said before, I know the numbers better than you ever will. But you
don't get it. You never slow down long enough to just listen."

"You're right. I don't. And that is definitely something I can grow
in. But is there a point while listening that I can ask questions?
Hard questions? I mean, hard for everyone, right? 'Cause the more
I learn, the more I've got them. A lot of them. And I think they're
honest ones, as best I can tell. I don't want to minimize your
experience, or anyone else's, or the broader realities of the age and
place we live in. I just want to be clear. Maybe just clear*er*. In my
heart and in my mind."

"Don't we all, Jons. Don't we all."

Another pause.

"Maybe," she tossed him the ball. "Just maybe, once I'm healed
up. You might be worth another shot," she offered. "But you are for
sure gonna need to work on that drop step."

Carter took it in, sending the ball back to her and feeling the
slightest bit more hopeful.

Bradford stepped toward her gear on the sideline. "But, Mae?"
she turned back slightly. "I like her for sure. Definitely married up,
Jons."

"See?" Carter laughed. "Already something we can agree on."

One of the best parts of writing stories is interacting with readers. Join my no-spam reader's newsletter and receive an exclusive, free ebook | audio book of Juarez Liberty - the prequel to the Zeb Dalton Thrillers. Just head over to waynecstewart.com, scroll to the bottom of the page and sign up. Looking forward to hearing from you.

FROM THE AUTHOR

Every story is birthed from within a context. This story garnered its first breaths from a few different sources. First, this last year our church went through the book of Nehemiah. I was reminded there of God's faithfulness, even when all seems darkest, and the call to faithfulness in every arena of life, especially that of public concern. Second, I have been thoroughly enjoying a podcast by my former pastor (Mike Woodruff - Christ Church Illinois). His unique way of framing history, current events, big ideas, and Scripture is an incredibly helpful primer on how to approach complexity in humility. Third, I recently ran across brief statements from Liz Forkin-Bohannan, urging us toward the power of small dreams and the close-proximity localization of real change.

Finally, I have in the last year found myself increasingly dissatisfied with my own reactions to the swirl of anger and discontent around us. I have opinions. I believe my opinions are rooted in God's truth but I also long to live them out in the kindness and love of God. So I feel most like I've done good work when my writing reflects even adverse opinions to mine in—what I dearly hope is—a fair and thoughtful manner. Is it too much to hope that a good story could help us remember our common image bearing identity and start from there? I am praying the answer is no. And that you found this to be a good story.

January 2023
Wayne C Stewart